LOVE SPELLS & LATE FEES

A LIBRARY WITCH MYSTERY

ELLE ADAMS

"Sylvester, stay away from the balloons!" shouted Estelle.

A heart-shaped balloon floated past, pursued by the huge tawny owl. With less than a week to go before Valentine's Day, bright pink ribbons adorned the library's shelves and festooned the balconies, and a bright box for Cupid's Card Delivery Service sat beside the desk at the front.

As the balloons ascended past the four storeys of towering shelves, Sylvester's beak pierced one of them with a deafening bang, and heart-shaped glittering pink confetti rained down on our heads.

"Those are supposed to be decorations," Estelle said in exasperated tones.

"They're also an unholy abomination." Cass pulled a handful of confetti out of her long curly red hair and dumped it on the desk.

"You might at least pretend to be supportive," her

sister said. "Can't you at least help me put the balloons away?"

Another bang came from above our heads, and Sylvester flew past, cackling.

I pulled out my wand and cast a quick levitation spell, sending the balloons flying upwards and away from the owl.

Sylvester, however, had other ideas. As the levitation spell caught the balloons, he spread his wings, generating an air current that sent several of them floating out of the open window.

"No!" Estelle cursed and ran for the door, throwing an angry gesture at the owl. I reached the door first, pulling out my Biblio-Witch Inventory.

Wands were one way of casting magic, but my family had another—the power of words. I reached for the page and tapped the word *fly* with my fingertip, and at once, the balloons changed direction and soared back towards the library.

Estelle caught up to me, breathless, and added her own magic on top of mine. As the balloons floated back into the lobby, Sylvester descended on them again.

"Stop that!" Estelle said. "Leave the balloons alone. You're making a complete mess of the place."

"I'm simply ridding the world of those monstrous things," he said. "Nobody wants pink heart-shaped balloons *or* confetti."

"For once we're in agreement," said Cass.

"Cass, not everyone agrees," said Estelle. "You kept saying we needed to fill our social calendar."

"Not with this kind of sappy nonsense," said Cass. "It's

making me want to give up dating altogether and move to live at the North Pole."

"Then you can organise your own Singles Awareness night instead if you like," Estelle said to her sister. "Or you can take charge of wrangling that menace of an owl."

The door to the library opened and a tall guy wearing a pair of bright pink wings walked into the library. Harris Jones, aka the library's very own Cupid, carried a fake bow and arrows strapped to his back which he wore while delivering cards. Only a broke student would suffer the indignity of dressing up in a silly costume to make a bit of cash, but the new service proved surprisingly popular. People from all over town came here to leave their notes for Cupid to deliver to the objects of their admiration, and every day, he'd come and collect the letters and take them to their intended targets.

"Am I likely to get chased again today?" Harris asked Estelle. "Yesterday, Roy James got mad at me and chased me all the way down the high street. I had to hide in the costume shop for half an hour, pretending to be part of the display."

"Sorry," said Estelle. "Occupational hazard of the job, I'm afraid, Harris."

He gave the bucket of cards a rueful shake and walked out of the library. "I wish these came with warning labels, so I knew who was likely to blow up at me. Still, this pays better than delivering newspapers."

The door closed behind him, and Estelle tutted. "Poor guy."

"He must have known what he was getting into," said Cass. "Not everyone can have it as perfect as Rory, for instance."

I rolled my eyes. Cass and I had never exactly been the best of friends, but she'd begun to warm to me a little in the last couple of months. When I'd first moved to the library, she'd maintained a steady grudge against my dad for walking out on the magical world to marry my mother, but she seemed to have accepted that I'd be sticking around for the long haul.

"My life is not perfect," I said. "Are you forgetting the reason we even have those balloons is because I accidentally set them loose from that second-floor corridor along with a plague of ghosts?"

The ghosts, thankfully, were long gone, but the balloons hadn't always been cute, heart-shaped and filled with confetti. When we'd originally found them, they'd been shaped like clawed and winged monsters, and while Estelle had transformed them into a more innocuous design, I wouldn't put it past Aunt Candace to sneakily turn them back into monsters when nobody was looking.

"Whatever," said Cass. "You're dating the Reaper."

"I am," I said. "He's also coming over to dinner later this week, and I think he'd be a little freaked out at all the pink confetti."

Cass snorted. "Why's he coming to dinner here? We've already met him. If anything, it's his turn to invite you to have dinner with the Grim Reaper."

"You know the Reaper doesn't actually need to eat, don't you?" I pointed out.

"Then why's he bothering to come here?" said Cass.

"Because it's polite," I told her. "And because Aunt Adelaide kept asking me to invite him."

In truth, I'd rather go on a date with him alone than put him through the indignity of a family gathering. He'd already met my family, though having all of them in the same room at the same time was a rare occurrence. Perhaps oddly, Xavier was the one who insisted on doing all the typical 'dating' stuff despite being further from the land of the living than I was.

"You'd better hope he doesn't get called out on Reaper duty again," she added.

"It's not like we can plan our schedule around people's deaths." Half our dates were cut short because Xavier was called out on Reaper duty—in other words, escorting a departed soul into the afterlife. I doubted the Grim Reaper even knew Valentine's Day was a thing, either. Dealing with the dead didn't allow much time for the living.

"Don't say that in front of Aunt Candace," Estelle said. "She'll put it in a book."

"And you wonder why I haven't invited him here yet." I gave an eye-roll.

"You haven't *asked* him yet?" Cass said. "He doesn't know he's coming here?"

I shrugged. "He's been busy."

"Can't you just text him?" she said. "You're the one who talked him into getting a mobile phone to begin with."

"Yeah, but the signal in the cemetery is almost as bad as here in the library."

"Too many dead people?" She gave another snort. "I think you're making excuses."

Maybe I was, but while Xavier and I had been officially dating for just over a month, part of me still expected the Grim Reaper to retract his promise to leave us in peace. For all I knew, inviting Xavier to an official meeting with my family might be a step too far. His boss still seemed to be under the impression this was just a temporary fling, and while I knew Xavier himself thought differently, one did not defy the Grim Reaper without facing the consequences.

The mobile phone was a definite plus. Admittedly, Xavier's new phone was a brick-like design from the early 2000s which could double as a paperweight, but at least Xavier and I had some means of contacting one another now. But asking the Reaper to dinner with my eccentric family? That wasn't the same as him taking me to a fancy restaurant or a walk on the beach. My family would come armed with a full array of awkward questions, most of which would be more awkward for me than for him. The guy was pretty laid-back for someone who made a career out of escorting the dead into the afterlife.

Aunt Candace walked into the lobby, her long black cloak flowing behind her and her hair in its usual bird's nest of tangled red curls.

"What is this ghastly mess?" she remarked of the heart-shaped confetti scattered all over the lobby floor.

"Told you so," said Cass. "You're outvoted, Estelle."

"You all voted in favour when I asked if I should put confetti in the balloons," said Estelle. "Look, it's supposed to fit the theme. Would you rather I made it in the shape of kelpies or unicorns?"

"Yes," said Cass. "I'm heading up to the pet shop. Don't bring in any more balloons while I'm gone."

"Please don't come back with a unicorn," Estelle called after her as she walked out of the library.

I dropped my voice. "I'm surprised she hasn't brought one here yet."

"Nah, even Cass wouldn't go that far," she said. "Animals like that aren't meant to be kept in captivity, besides. I bet she's just off to buy food for her pets."

"I don't mind the heart-shaped balloons, for the record," I added, "but it's your judgement call."

"Unicorn-shaped balloons might work," she said thoughtfully. "Aunt Candace, aren't you going to chip in? I know you have some ideas."

"This theme," she said, gesturing to the bright pink confetti, "is not my thing."

"Better than one of your atmospheric writing sessions," Estelle said. "Just because you're writing a dark and stormy night scene doesn't mean everyone else needs to experience it as well."

"I had to get the right ambience."

"Not *inside* the library," said Estelle. "Nobody wants to get rained on."

"If they didn't, they wouldn't live on the coast of England," said Aunt Candace. "Besides, you're the one covering the place in glitter."

"There's not *that* much." Estelle brushed pink glitter from her cloak. "Maybe a little."

"A little?" Aunt Adelaide walked up to join us. "I found some in my bed earlier."

"Sorry, Mum."

Aunt Adelaide, Estelle's mother, shared her curvy figure and the same red hair as the rest of us had, while her cloak bore the silver emblem of our family—an owl and two pens crossed. "Aside from the glitter, how are the preparations going?"

"It'd be going better if Sylvester didn't keep attacking

my balloons," said Estelle. "Cupid just left to deliver today's letters."

"Is he the kid in the silly costume?" said Aunt Candace. "You know, the original Cupid didn't wear those ridiculous fairy wings."

"It's not supposed to be an accurate representation of the Greek legend," Estelle said. "What would you rather he wear, nothing?"

"I didn't know Valentine's Day was even a thing in the magical world, let alone Cupid," I remarked. "How do you pick which human traditions to follow?"

"It varies," said Aunt Adelaide. "All magical communities are different. As for Cupid… I believe the idea of dressing up in a costume with wings originated when a particular magical community hired fairies to deliver their letters. Somehow, the tradition merged with the Greek legend, and this was the result."

"I guess it's appropriate, given that fairies can make you fall in love with a snap of their fingers," said Estelle. "Hmm… maybe I should use fairy-shaped confetti instead of hearts."

Aunt Candace gave a snort. "If you're looking for an idea for a new event, Hayley Sutton is running a blind dating service at the city hall."

"I know she is," said Estelle. "Are you thinking of giving it a try?"

"I am," said Aunt Adelaide. "I signed up myself this week. I have a date this Friday."

"Ooh," said Aunt Candace. "Do tell."

"I'm not giving you any material to use in your books," said Aunt Adelaide firmly. "And I'm not saying where, either. This is the first date I've had in weeks and I won't have you frightening off my date by writing him into a book."

"Oh, you know I never use real people in my books," said Aunt Candace.

I cleared my throat. "And my dad's life story ended up being fictionalised by accident?"

"He gave permission," she said indignantly. "Really. If you're going to be like that, I'll sign up to the blind dating service myself."

"If you're looking for ideas, why not ask Cupid instead?" Estelle said. "He's been dealing with scorned lovers all week while delivering Valentine's cards to people. I'm sure he'll have a few stories to share. Anonymous, of course."

"Did you offer him hazard pay?" Aunt Candace walked away, brushing glitter off her cloak as she did so. "I may take you up on that offer, if that crow of yours runs out of gossip."

"Honestly." Aunt Adelaide frowned after her sister. "If she does sign up, we'd better not end up going to the same place for our dates."

She and her husband had amicably divorced when Cass and Estelle were younger, while Aunt Candace's last relationship had been her ill-fated fling with Dominic, a vampire who'd died shortly after their breakup when he'd run afoul of a thief. Aunt Candace was already writing a book featuring the two of them as star-crossed lovers, and while Dominic wasn't alive to challenge her, she was better off making up her own stories than dragging real people into them. Then again, she was hardly the only member of our family to have a love life strange and eventful enough to be immortalised in one of her novels. Look at me and the Reaper.

"I feel sorry for whoever she ends up on a blind date with," I said. "She'll have her notebook out there and then, I don't doubt."

"Everyone knows her by reputation at least," said Estelle. "They'll know what they're getting into."

"I suppose you're right." I shook confetti off my cloak. "Also, I don't think Cass and Aunt Candace should be taken as speaking for the majority. Most people like the decorations."

The library was an impressive enough sight in its default state, with five stories of towering shelves climbing up to the high ceiling, balconies overlooking the ground floor, and pretty lanterns which switched on in the evenings. Our family's living quarters lay through a corridor on our left-hand side, while more doors further back led into classrooms and locked areas for the more dangerous of the library's books. Life in a magical library was nothing if not exciting.

"They won't if Sylvester bursts all the balloons and terrifies everyone," she pointed out. "Maybe I should shut him in an upper corridor."

"Or find him a date."

She laughed. "What, another owl?"

That's more likely than finding another embodiment of the library's entire store of knowledge. Not that anyone except for me knew of Sylvester's true nature. It wouldn't surprise me if he was unique in the magical world. He certainly acted as though he was. "Maybe."

Her eyes sparked. "I could set up a blind dating service for familiars. I was actually talking to Alice from the pet shop about that the other day. I reckon it'd be popular with the other witches."

"Can you imagine how Sylvester would react around the other familiars, though?" I said. "He'd terrify everyone."

"Maybe Jet wants to meet another crow. I'll add it to the list." She whipped out a notebook and scribbled a note down.

Nothing made Estelle happier than organising events. There was a reason she was head of hospitality at the library. I was happier in a behind-the-scenes role, but Estelle and I had become close friends when I'd moved into the library and of my new family members, she and I had the most in common. We both enjoyed studying, though Estelle was doing a PhD in practical magical skills while I'd only joined the magical world about three months ago. While I'd passed both Grade Two and Three of my magical training, I was still an apprentice biblio-witch with a lot to learn.

Despite all that, I'd come a long way in a short space of time. I'd even claimed my dad's old wand, thought lost for years, and I'd done far braver things than asking the Reaper to dinner since my induction into the magical world.

My phone buzzed with a message. I retrieved it from my pocket, expecting the text to be from Xavier, but instead it was from Laney, who'd been my best friend since before I'd moved to the library.

Are you doing anything fun on Valentine's Day?

I rarely thought of my old life before the library these days, except when Laney messaged me. While I'd alluded to my new relationship in my messages to her, telling her

I was dating the angel of death would not be a good idea. And not just because telling normals about the magical world was frowned upon at best. Still, I hated lying to someone who'd once been the only friend I'd had.

I think I'll have a date, I responded.

With the dreamy guy you like? When can I meet him?

I hesitated to respond. While mentioning Xavier was the one way I could keep my best friend updated on my new life without having to lie, having her meet him in person was something else entirely. I'd need to think about that one.

"Danger!" yelled a shrill voice. My crow familiar, Jet, tapped on the window from the inside.

Frowning, I walked over to him. "What is it?"

Estelle dropped the notebook on the desk and hurried to join me. "What's the issue?"

"Something outside, I think." I moved to the oak doors leading outside and pushed them open.

On the doorstep, Cupid lay flat on his back, an arrow sticking out of his shoulder. Silence fell as Estelle crouched over his body for a moment, then straightened upright.

"He won't wake up," she said tremulously. "I think he's dead."

2

Cupid lay sprawled on the steps, his wings splayed at odd angles and the arrows from his costume scattered all over the ground.

"Did anyone see who did it?" I scanned the town square, of which the library covered an entire side, but it was before nine in the morning and few people were outside. "Was it one of his own arrows they shot him with?"

"It *looks* the same," Estelle said. "I'll call the police."

As she ducked back into the library, I had little choice but to stay beside the body on the steps and cross my fingers that the square stayed deserted until the police showed up. Estelle had wanted to draw more business to the library, but a dead body on the doorstep wasn't what any of us had had in mind.

Jet flew down to land on my shoulder. "Arrows!"

"Did you see who did it?" I asked my familiar.

"No, partner," he said solemnly. "Is he dead?"

"I think so." I drew in a breath. "Can you fly around

town and tell me if you see anyone carrying arrows or otherwise acting suspiciously?"

"Of course, partner!" He took flight in a beat of wings, the undercurrent of air lifting the hair from my forehead. A rattling noise sounded as one of the arrows tumbled down the steps onto the ground.

Hang on a second. There was no blood on the arrow that'd hit Cupid, nor any visible signs of an injury—and besides, the arrows were props bought from a costume shop. They shouldn't be able to deal someone a fatal wound.

"I don't think he's dead." I called over my shoulder. "Estelle?"

No answer. She must already be on the phone to the police. I pushed open the door to the library and called, "Aunt Adelaide? Can you help me out here?"

My aunt hurried into view. "Someone was shot, Estelle said. Who is he?"

"Harris Jones. The guy we hired as Cupid." I indicated his sprawling body. "Look at the arrows. They aren't real."

Aunt Adelaide crouched down beside Harris, while I took his wrist in my hand, feeling the unmistakable flutter of a pulse. "He *is* alive."

"Estelle!" Aunt Adelaide called. "Were there any witnesses, do you know?"

"I sent Jet to scout around." I pointed to the dark shape of the little crow flying over the town square.

"Those arrows aren't sharp enough to cause more than a papercut." Aunt Adelaide carefully picked one of them up. "Unless magic was involved."

Estelle reappeared in the doorway, her phone in her hand. "Did you say he wasn't dead?"

"Someone spelled him," said Aunt Adelaide. "Or spelled the arrows, at any rate."

"He *looks* dead." Estelle climbed down the steps alongside Harris's body. "Which is the arrow that hit him?"

"That one." I pointed to the arrow that lay across his chest. "The arrow must have been spelled, or they wouldn't have been able to do any damage by stabbing him with it."

Estelle crouched beside him and lifted the arrow, holding it up to examine it closer. When I peered at the edge, it became clear that a bright pink liquid stained the arrow tip. "There's some kind of potion on it," she said, "but I already told Edwin he was dead. He'll be on his way here."

"Since he's not dead, we should get him off the doorstep before people start gossiping," said Aunt Adelaide.

She pulled out her wand and gave it a flick, levitating Harris's body through the open doors into the library. Estelle and I hastened to gather the arrows, depositing them on the front desk while Aunt Adelaide laid Harris down on the carpet in the lobby. He didn't move or speak, and his eyes remained closed. No wonder Estelle and I had mistaken him for dead.

"How do we wake him up?" I flicked through my Biblio-Witch Inventory, though I hadn't started learning how to undo complicated spells in my lessons yet.

Aunt Adelaide scrutinised Harris's body. "You can try a reversal spell, but if the potion is powerful, it'll require a specialist antidote."

Estelle pulled out her own Biblio-Witch Inventory and tapped a word, but Harris didn't stir. I peered over her shoulder as she pressed her fingertip to the word *wake,* but again, there was no change.

"Let's see if it works if we both do it at the same time." I grabbed the plain notebook I kept in my pocket and turned to a blank page. "Ready?"

I pressed my pen to the notepad at the same time as Estelle readied herself to use her Biblio-Witch Inventory again. Then I wrote the word, *wake.*

Harris's eyelids didn't so much as flutter. Aunt Adelaide pursed her lips. "As I thought. A simple spell wouldn't have such a strong effect on him, but he's out cold."

"That, or I need more training." I returned the pen and notebook to my pocket. Every time I thought I was making strides in my magical education, another reminder of something I hadn't covered yet came along and made me feel like an amateur again.

"What've you done now?" Cass entered the library, a bag from the familiar shop in one hand and an arrow in the other.

"Cass," said Estelle. "Did you go to extreme measures to stop Cupid delivering?"

"What?" Cass dropped the arrow on the desk alongside the others. "What are you talking about? I found this on the doorstep."

"Someone put a potion on one of the arrows before using it to stab our Cupid," I explained. "Harris is unconscious, and we thought he was dead."

"Who…" Cass's gaze fell on the sleeping body of Harris Jones. "You think *I* did that to him? I can't believe you'd even suggest that."

"It was a joke," said Estelle. "You've been talking about how stupid his costume is all week."

"It *is* stupid." Cass headed for the entryway into our family's living quarters. "I'm not surprised someone objected to it so much that they decided to shoot the messenger."

Estelle approached the desk. "We should make sure the other arrows aren't covered in the potion, too. Maybe they can give us a clue about what kind of potion was used on him."

"Before that, we'll move him," said Aunt Adelaide. "We open in less than an hour. I can't imagine our patrons will want to be greeted by an unconscious Cupid."

"He didn't even get around to delivering the letters," Estelle said ruefully, reaching into his pocket and pulling out a wad of envelopes.

"Deal with those later," said Aunt Adelaide. "I'll take the arrows. You two, take Harris into the Reading Corner and wait for the police to show up."

Estelle and I levitated Harris onto a vacant sofa at the back of the ground floor. The Reading Corner was a cosy area containing hammocks, beanbags and comfy seats, surrounded by shelves lined with well-thumbed volumes of escapist fiction. For that reason, it was among my favourite hangouts in the library, and one of the few places which stayed relatively predictable by the library's standards.

"Don't worry," I said to Estelle. "I'm sure your mum will get to the bottom of this. She's knowledgeable and experienced."

In the unlikely event that she couldn't find the answer,

there was always the Book of Questions. But that wouldn't tell us *who* had shot Cupid, and why.

She exhaled in a sigh. "I know, but I can't figure out why someone would choose to stab him with one of his own arrows. They must have taken the arrow from him and *then* dipped it in the potion."

"They must have had a good shot, then, or they were standing at close range," I commented. "Which makes it weirder that they disappeared so fast."

"They might not have." She sat down on a beanbag. "He was lying out there for a good ten minutes before I thought to look outside."

"Don't blame yourself," I said. "I didn't think to look, either. You don't expect Cupid to get shot by one of his own arrows, do you?"

Estelle picked up a handful of confetti from the floor of the Reading Corner. "Between this and Sylvester, it'll be lucky if anyone shows up to the poetry night special on Monday."

"We have enough time to turn this around." It was usually Estelle who reassured me, not the other way around, but she'd put so much time and effort into organising the week's events that I hated to see it ruined. "Just ask for another volunteer to play Cupid."

"Without mentioning what happened to the last one," Estelle added. "But he won't be able to name the person who shot him until we can figure out how to undo whatever potion they used on him."

"There's got to be a counter-spell or cure which can wake him up," I said. "Aunt Adelaide will be able to figure it out if neither of us can."

"Mm." She glanced at the door. "I hope so. Who would even do this?"

"Didn't he say someone chased him around yesterday after a bad breakup?" I asked. "Maybe they were hoping he'd sleep through Valentine's Day altogether."

Her eyes widened. "I should have paid more attention. I didn't realise people would be this antagonistic over Valentine's cards."

The sound of the door opening echoed throughout the ground floor. "There's Edwin."

We reached the front desk to find the elf policeman had entered the library, accompanied by his two troll guards. The elf looked unintimidating compared to his two bodyguards, but their brutish muscles belied their affable natures. One of them—a tall grey-skinned troll named Rocky—gave me a cheery wave, and I waved back.

"You claimed there was a body on your doorstep," the elf said. "Where is he?"

"He's over here, but he's not dead." I beckoned him to the Reading Corner. "Our Cupid was shot by one of his own arrows, spiked with some kind of potion that sent him into a coma. We brought him indoors when we realised that he was still alive."

Estelle walked into step with Edwin. "I panicked when I found his body and forgot to check for a pulse, but he's definitely alive."

Edwin and his two troll guards walked with us through the library to the spot where Harris lay. The chief of police leaned over his sleeping body. "What kind of potion was it?"

"Aunt Adelaide is running tests on the arrow he was shot with to figure it out," I explained. "We don't think the shooter intended to kill him, but that's all we know so far."

"Were there any witnesses?" he asked.

"Not that I'm aware of," I said. "My familiar spotted him lying outside the window. Estelle, Aunt Adelaide and I were in the library and didn't hear anything outside."

"Ah, Edwin." Aunt Adelaide approached us, an arrow in her hand. "I identified the potion they used on the arrow. It's called Poison Apple. Very strong stuff. I expect he'll be unconscious for as long as it takes to brew the antidote, but when he wakes up, he'll be able to identify who shot him."

"Poison Apple?" I said. "What, you mean like from Snow White?"

"Poison?" echoed Edwin. "Is this a homicide or not?"

"Despite the name, it's rarely fatal," she said. "However, Poison Apple puts the victim into a deep sleep until an antidote is found. Unfortunately, it has only one antidote, and it's a complex one to make. I'd give it at least a few days to brew."

"If that's the case, I will let the boy's parents know," said Edwin. "And I will put out a call for witnesses. Is he the boy who's been delivering cards for the last few days?"

"He is," I said. "I heard he had trouble with some of the people he delivered cards to, so it's possible one of them reacted badly."

"Yes, I heard he delivered a private note from a were-ferret to a wererabbit which caused the entire local were-ferret pack to declare a feud against the wererabbit's chief," he said. "They met through the blind dating service. Was that here in the library?"

"The blind dating service?" I echoed. "That's not ours.

Estelle is organising the card delivery, but it's Hayley Sutton who set up the blind dating service at the town hall. Do you think this wereferret might have been angry enough with Cupid to want to take him out of the picture?"

"It's not my place to judge," he said, pulling out his phone. "I will call the boy's family."

He walked away from the Reading Corner, while his troll guards left the library through the front doors, perhaps to look around for potential witnesses. I didn't believe anybody who worked in the town square would have seen Harris being shot, otherwise they'd have let us know. The other shops were too far away from the library to be in with a clear view, and even if the shooter had hidden inside one of them, he'd be long gone by now.

Aunt Adelaide made a quick call, too, then returned to join us in the Reading Corner. "The hospital doesn't have any master alchemists on staff, so they're looking into their options. That potion is notoriously difficult to craft and even harder to counter. My guess is that they'll have to bring in a specialist."

"Did the person who made the Poison Apple brew it themselves?" I asked. "Because if it's that hard to do, then surely that narrows the list of possible suspects."

"True," said Estelle. "But—if he's unconscious for days, how is he supposed to tell us who did it?"

"He isn't," said Aunt Adelaide. "I'll see what the local alchemists say. Can one of you keep an eye on the front desk?"

"Tell you what, I'll leave a sign up saying the library's closed until noon," said Estelle, resigned. "It's better than having people walk in and out of here with Harris lying here looking like he's dead."

Edwin returned, a harried expression on his face. "Adelaide, I'll have to take that arrow, as evidence."

"Fine, but make sure nobody touches the end of it," she said. "We don't need anyone else rendered comatose."

"No, we certainly do not." He carefully took the arrow from her between his fingertips. "I heard what you said about the hospital. Do any of the books here in the library contain the recipe for the antidote?"

"We certainly have a number of books containing that information," said Aunt Adelaide. "However, potions aren't my speciality. That's more my sister's area. I'll speak to her."

"Good luck with that," Estelle said in an undertone. "If I were you, I'd hire an alchemist instead."

"I guess we're going to need to hire a new Cupid, too," I added.

"I have a few people on reserve," said Estelle. "It was a fairly popular idea before it all started to go wrong."

"I suppose the generous pay makes up for being chased by angry romantically scorned people," I said. "But—is the new Cupid going to want to go ahead with it after what happened to the last guy? I'm not sure we'll be able to keep this quiet."

Estelle's face fell. "Good point."

"What's going on?" Aunt Candace walked out of the family's living quarters. At once, her gaze went to Harris's unconscious body. "What did you do? Bore him to sleep?"

"He's in a coma," said Estelle. "Someone shot him with one of his own arrows."

"Doesn't look like he's been shot to me." As usual, a

pen hovered at Aunt Candace's side, scribbling away in a floating notebook. "What did they shoot him with?"

"The arrow was spiked with a potion," said Estelle. "Poison Apple, my mum said."

"How unfortunate," said Aunt Candace. "Someone got angry over his love notes, did they?"

"So it seems," said Aunt Adelaide. "You still have those books on how to brew up antidotes for strong sleeping potions in your research cave, don't you?"

"Yes, I do," she said. "Why, are you asking *me* to brew you a cure?"

"If we can't find anyone else," said Aunt Adelaide. "I will continue checking the other arrows to see if they might be covered in the same potion, or if the shooter left any traces of their identity behind."

"Excuse me?" said Aunt Candace. "You can't find anyone to brew this cure for you aside from me?"

"It's a specialist job," said her sister. "One that would normally be entrusted to a master alchemist, but since young Harris was our employee and we have the skills, it would be remiss of us to leave him to struggle alone."

"Really?" said Aunt Candace. "If that's the case, then let's talk compensation."

The two of them walked away, heads bent to talk to one another, leaving Estelle and me with Harris's inert sleeping form.

"I can't believe my mum thinks Aunt Candace will be able to help," she whispered. "I know it's a difficult antidote to brew, but if anything, that's a good reason *not* to get her involved. The last time she cooked dinner, she left a steak at the bottom of the oven for three days."

"Better hope they find someone else, then," I said.

"Problem is, everyone knows master alchemists charge a small fortune," she added. "And we need Harris awake so he can name the culprit. You're right about the next Cupid being a potential target. Not sure what to do about that."

"Ask Sylvester to be their bodyguard?" I suggested.

She snorted. "Sylvester? He'd peck you half to death for asking."

"You aren't wrong." I glanced around, and startled at the sight of a blond figure standing by the desk. "Ah. We have company."

Xavier. Considering he was the Reaper, you'd think I'd find him standing beside dead bodies more often, not the other way around. He caught my eye and smiled, gliding across the floor in his typical Reaper fashion. Seeing him always cheered me up, despite the scythe strapped to his back and the knowledge that yet another near-dead body had come between us.

"Hey," I said. "You're not here to collect a soul, are you?"

"I wasn't certain on that one." He indicated Harris's sleeping body. "I heard someone died here, but he's clearly not dead."

"I know he isn't," I said. "He's in a coma thanks to a powerful sleeping draught someone put on one of his own arrows."

"Arrows?" He looked closer, eyeing the crumpled wings strapped to Harris's back. "That's the guy you hired to play Cupid, right?"

"You've got it," I said. "Let's just say there's a fair few people in town who'd have good reason to want to put an end to his delivery service, and one of them went a step too far and shot him."

"Oh," he said. "Sorry I barged in, but I heard Edwin's troll guards talking about a death and wondered why I hadn't been called to collect their soul. If he's in a deep sleep, it's an easy mistake to make."

"You don't need to apologise for coming here," I said. "I always appreciate your company."

"I'm afraid there's not much I can do to help if he isn't dead," he said. "Is there a cure for the sleeping potion? I assume there is."

"There is, but it's a difficult antidote to brew," I said. "My aunts are looking into the options while we wait for his family to come here."

"Edwin's trolls are walking around the town square," he added. "Are they looking for the culprit?"

"Whoever it was, nobody spotted him except Harris himself, and he's likely to be asleep for days," I said. "When he wakes up, he'll be able to set the record straight, hopefully without needing your boss to get involved."

"I'd prefer to keep him out of it." He moved in closer, his startlingly bright aquamarine eyes more vivid than any human eyes I'd seen. "Are we still on for tonight's date?"

"Of course." I leaned into his embrace, and he pulled me tight against him. I could feel my heart thumping, and the silence where his own heartbeat would have been. The world blanked out in a wave of happy bliss as I kissed him for a moment that didn't last nearly long enough.

He released me. "I'll see you in a couple of hours, all right?"

"See you soon, Reaper!" Aunt Candace cooed, walking across the lobby as Xavier glided back towards the door.

I scowled at her. "Aren't you meant to be calling up someone to brew an antidote?"

"Not at all." She drew herself upright in a proud manner. "I have been tasked with brewing the antidote myself, as I have considerable experience in brewing sleeping potions."

"You're doing it yourself?" Aunt Adelaide must have faith in her ability to pull it off, then.

"There's no need to sound so surprised," said Aunt Candace. "Do tell me if he turns out to be dead after all. I'd hate to waste my limited free time on a pointless task."

And with that, she sauntered away. Shaking my head, I went back to re-join Estelle beside Harris's body.

"Going well, is it?" she said. "With Xavier, I mean?"

"It is," I said. "As long as we don't get interrupted during tonight's date again—"

With a deafening bang, the door slammed open, and a tall, fearsome woman walked into the library. Estelle and I both jumped upright when the stranger marched through the library and halted beside the Reading Corner.

"What did you do to my son?" bellowed the woman.

Uh-oh. "Are you Harris's mother?" said Estelle.

"Of course I am," she snapped. "First he has to deal with that low-life girl dumping him and breaking his heart, and now someone has poisoned my boy."

"He'll wake up," I said consolingly. "He isn't poisoned, he's asleep."

Aunt Adelaide hurried over to us, dropping several arrows as she did so. "You must be Mrs Jones. We found an antidote for the sleeping potion which can wake your son, but it's incredibly expensive to brew. You can hire a specialist, or if you'd prefer, we'll do it ourselves—"

"Because he was attacked on your property," she finished. "Do you think I'd pay some second-rate alchemist to brew it? Get me that antidote right away."

Aunt Adelaide cleared her throat. "I'm afraid the cure will take several days to brew, but your son will make a full recovery."

"Days?" she snapped, so loudly that several books jumped on their shelves. "Unbelievable. This was supposed to be a safe part-time job, this was. I expected better of the library."

"I'm sorry," said Estelle. "Would you like—"

"I don't want anything except my son back," she said. "I'm taking him home."

Ignoring my aunt's and Estelle's protests, she lifted Cupid's limp body over her shoulder and carried him through the lobby. As she reached the door, one of his wings fell off and flopped onto the carpet.

Estelle pressed a hand to her forehead. "I can't make the cure brew faster just because she wants it to. The person who did this wanted him to sleep straight through Valentine's day. There's no way around it."

"I know," I said. "Ignore her. You're doing your best. And we'll have the cure ready soon, one way or another."

Aunt Adelaide walked over to the door and picked up the discarded wing. "Yes, well. If she doesn't want to buy it from an apothecary—and I wouldn't if I were her, considering the cost—we'll have to hope nothing distracts Candace this week."

"We'll keep her on track," said Estelle. "Hey—Jet's back."

The little crow flew back into the library, landed on my shoulder and nuzzled my ear affectionately. "Hey, Jet."

"I didn't find anyone," said the crow. "No arrows, nothing."

"No worries," I said. "Whoever shot Harris had time to hide. It took us too long to find him, and I think it's a good job you were looking out the window, otherwise it'd have taken longer. Did you see anyone else acting suspiciously?"

"No, partner," he said. "But I heard a rumour in town that a jealous ex-lover of his shot Cupid dead."

"He's not dead," I said. "Can you fly around and listen out to hear if there's been any particularly nasty breakups this week? Or if anyone might have had another reason to target Cupid?"

"Of course, partner!"

He took flight again in a sweep of wings. My crow familiar always knew the latest gossip, so I had little doubt he'd be able to help us assemble a list of suspects. We had to start somewhere.

Estelle sighed. "I'd better put up the ad for a new Cupid. We'll open the library for the day in the meantime."

"Poor Estelle's putting herself under pressure over this," said Aunt Adelaide, as her daughter walked away. "And I can hardly blame her."

"Someone has already started a rumour that a jealous ex-lover of Cupid's was responsible for shooting him," I said.

"Of course they would," she said. "Pay it no attention."

"What about the arrows?" I asked. "Were any of the others covered in the same potion?"

"Not that I can tell," she said. "This was planned, all

right, but an attack on Cupid isn't the same as an attack on the library. Estelle knows that."

"I know," I said. "We're talking about the same person who pulled a fancy ball together at the last minute while most of the town was under a spell. She has this in hand."

I hope. Now all I had to do was make it to my date with Xavier this evening without running into any more dead or almost-dead bodies. Oh, and prepare to ask him to come to dinner with my family. No pressure.

3

Xavier and I had been to the Black Dog several times before, and it had swiftly become my favourite seafront pub. We chatted over fish and chips, and it was a relief to put all thoughts of Cupid, Mrs Jones and jealous ex-lovers shooting people with arrows to the back of my mind.

More difficult was trying to find an opportune moment to ask Xavier to come to dinner with my family. In the end, during a lull in our conversation, I blurted, "Do you want to meet my family? I mean—I know you've already met them, but I wondered if you'd like to come and have dinner with us one day this week."

"Sure." He smiled. "Anytime."

"Fair warning," I added, "I can't pretend my family won't make it into an uncomfortable experience. Aunt Candace still keeps threatening to write our story into a book."

"I deal with dead people screaming at me on a regular basis," he commented. "I think I can handle your family."

"Ah." Now I felt bad for doubting him. "I'm just not sure *I* can, sometimes. Though both my aunts are going on blind dates of their own this week, so maybe we'll be able to avoid being the centre of attention."

"Oh, they're using the blind dating service?" he said.

"Even you know about that?" I arched a brow. "Why, is the Grim Reaper trying it out?"

He grinned. "No, which is good news for the other participants. I just kept seeing posters around town advertising it."

"Yeah, the town's going all-out on the Valentine's theme." I dipped a chip in ketchup and transferred it to my mouth.

"Your cousin's hosting a bunch of events at the library, too, right?"

"She is," I said. "Though at the moment, Estelle is focused on finding another Cupid. I hope they aren't all put off by what happened to the last guy."

"I'm sure you'll find someone," he said. "As soon as your Cupid wakes up, he'll tell the police who was responsible."

"Yeah." I put down my fork. "I can't figure out who'd shoot someone over a Valentine's card, but some people seem pretty on edge this week."

"Passions run high for humans at this time of year, I've noticed," he commented.

"Speaking like… well, a Reaper."

He smiled at me across the table. "I never said I didn't have any passion of my own. It's just directed at one target."

My face heated up. "Oh."

He took my hand in his and laced our fingers together under the table. "I take it that was a positive 'oh'?"

"What else would it be?" A little thrill went through my bones whenever he touched me, even now. It seemed ridiculous that something so simple could make me so happy, but Xavier had seen in me what nobody else had. Despite all the obstacles life had thrown in our path, we were together, and I couldn't be happier.

———

The following morning dawned with a shower of glitter. Jet flew around my bed, shedding glitter, confetti and feathers everywhere.

"What did you do, fly into a balloon?" I picked a handful of confetti out of my hair, resigning myself to finding the stuff everywhere for the next couple of weeks.

"You told me to listen to the townspeople, so I did," he squeaked.

"Did you hear Harris's name mentioned in a negative light?" The crow might be enthusiastic, but he had considerable difficulty distinguishing useful information from rumours.

"A number of people arrived to express their condolences to the family," he said, "but Mrs Jones chased them out of the hospital with a broomstick!"

"I mean, did you get any idea about who might have shot him?" I asked. "Anyone he delivered cards to who went through nasty breakups in the last few weeks? Tell you what, go and find Estelle downstairs, and I'll get dressed and join you in a minute."

When I got downstairs, I found Estelle sitting at the

kitchen table eating cornflakes, a morose expression on her face. Jet perched in front of her, relating what sounded like every major breakup in town over the last month. *Oh, well, it was worth a shot.*

I grabbed a coffee mug and plate someone had kindly left out for me and joined her at the table. "Jet, calm down a moment. Did any of those people you mentioned have contact with Cupid?"

Estelle shot me an exasperated look. "You told him to listen out for gossip? You know what happened last time."

"I asked him to check if there was anyone who'd been through a breakup lately who might have a good reason to shoot Cupid." I sipped my coffee. "I figured he might overhear something useful."

"Isn't it more likely to be someone who knew Harris personally?" she asked.

"Maybe, but a lot of people were annoyed at the Valentine's cards," I said. "He mentioned someone chased him the day before yesterday, didn't he?"

Someone who went through a rough breakup, taking out their angst by shooting down Cupid. It wasn't an implausible theory.

"He did," she said. "I should have paid more attention."

"It's not your fault," I told her. "It was probably a jealous student who felt rejected. It's not worth beating yourself up over someone else's choice. You're doing a great job."

She gave a tentative smile. "Maybe, but in the meantime, we have no Cupid. Nobody has responded to the ad yet."

"I'm sure they will." An odd, pungent smell tickled my

nostrils, and I glanced over at the stove, where a cauldron simmered. "Is that the antidote?"

"Aunt Candace told me to watch it for the next half-hour." Estelle glanced over at the cauldron. "I hope she's paying attention to the timing. It's never been one of her strong points."

"Aunt Adelaide will keep her on the right track." I crossed the room and peered into the cauldron on the stove. A bright purple liquid simmered within, smelling strongly of herbs. I'd started basic potion classes a few weeks ago, but it'd be a long while before I learned anything that complex. "Aunt Candace is supposed to be giving me a lesson tomorrow, but I think I'd rather she forgot and remembered the antidote instead."

Especially if we wanted to avoid another visit from Mrs Jones.

Jet chattered away at Estelle and me as we set up the library for the day, telling me all about the town's romantic entanglements. It seemed half the town had used Hayley's blind dating service at the town hall, which explained why we'd had such an influx of people wanting Cupid to deliver cards. By the time we opened, Estelle was back to her usual bright and perky self, so I felt doubly motivated to get to the bottom of who'd shot Cupid and to ensure her Valentine's plans went ahead without a hitch.

An hour into my shift, a tall guy with red hair and freckles came up to the front desk. "I wondered if you could point me to a book on magical law enforcement? I tried asking the owl, but he led me into a dead end."

Really, Sylvester. "Sure, no problem."

I walked out from behind the desk and through the

stacks, and he followed behind me. "It's for my dissertation proposal."

"It's here on the ground floor." Then, inspired, I added, "Do you know Roy James?"

"Roy James?" he echoed. "Yeah, he's in my class. Why?"

"Our Cupid was put into a coma yesterday," I explained. "He said Roy chased after him the day before he was shot. I gathered he was angry about the Valentine's cards, so I wondered if we could talk to him."

"So that's where Harris went," said the student. "I'm not surprised, either. That guy has been stirring up trouble all week. For some people, anyway. I hired him to deliver a note to the guy I like, and he agreed to go on a date with me this weekend, so I can't say I have any complaints."

I filed that information away. "Is Roy in the library today?"

"He's over there." He pointed to a group of students at one of the tables near the Reading Corner. Now I looked more closely, a fair few students were here. While most of them were doing research for their dissertations, that particular group looked more like they were indulging in social drinking. *Oh, boy.*

"The book you need is that way." I pointed. "I'll deal with them."

He wandered off with a grunt of thanks, while I steeled myself for a potential confrontation. Walking over to the student's table, I put on my most authoritative voice. "No beer in the library."

"You don't make the rules," said a guy of around twenty or so, lounging on the desk with his feet propped on a chair.

"Technically, we do," I said. "Didn't you hear about the guy who left an open bottle of beer here in the library a few years ago and attracted a swarm of book moths which ate him alive?"

Sending a silent thanks to Aunt Candace for providing that story, I watched the whole group silently push their beer cans away. Looking slightly cowed, the guy I'd spoken to rose to his feet. "All right, I'll get rid of it."

"Also, which of you is Roy James?" I added. "Can I have a word, please?"

"Me." A guy with glasses and dreadlocks raised his hand. "What is it? The beer wasn't my idea."

"It's not about the beer." I beckoned him to follow me out of earshot of the others. "Did you hear about Harris Jones?"

"Who… the guy you had dressed up as Cupid?" he said. "In a coma, isn't he?"

"Yes," I said. "He was shot with an arrow while delivering letters for the library yesterday. I'm told you and he had a disagreement the other day."

He blinked. "You think *I* did it?"

"I wouldn't know," I said, "but so far, your name is the only one that's come up in connection with him. I'm told you chased him around and terrified him."

"That's an exaggeration," he said. "You know what he did, right? He cheated on his girlfriend with Laila Chen when he knew I'd asked her out. I think being in a coma for a few days will be good for him."

I tilted my head. "But you aren't confessing to using Poison Apple on him?"

"Poison Apple?" He snorted. "Where would I have got

my hands on that? The ingredients alone are worth my entire monthly budget."

I hadn't thought of the financial aspect. "Can *any* of the students afford a potion like that?"

"I don't know, but his girlfriend was angry with him for cheating," he said. "For all I know, she wanted payback herself, but I didn't do it, I swear."

"Who is this ex-girlfriend of his?" I asked.

"Carey Landon," he said. "She was really mad at him. Not only did he cheat on her, he also delivered a note to the person she'd planned to ask out this weekend and said some unflattering things so he cancelled their date."

"Ouch." I felt considerably less well-disposed towards Harris, if it was true. "Where might I find his ex?"

"She's Zee's new assistant at the bakery."

"Oh, good, she did hire someone new." I'd planned to make a quick run over there during my lunch break anyway. "If you're sure you don't have anything else to tell me, I'll leave it for now. But if you can think of anyone else who might have had a reason to take our Cupid out of the picture, we'd be grateful if you told us before we hire someone else."

"It's not the Cupid I have a problem with, it's Harris," he said. "If you're looking to hire someone else, pick someone who won't deliberately stir up trouble."

"I'll keep that in mind." I returned to the front desk, putting the Cupid issue to the back of my mind... for now.

When it was time for lunch, I headed across the square to Zee's place. The bakery was a large, bright shop with windows filled with rows of iced buns and cakes, pastries and cookies. If Harris's ex-girlfriend *had* been responsible for shooting him, it would have been easy for her to run into the bakery to hide before anyone spotted Harris's body, but I didn't know her well enough to accurately guess whether or not she'd been the one who'd shot him.

Zee, a black woman with braided hair and a friendly smile, wore an apron covered in a dusting of flour. Behind her stood a young blond student who wore red-framed glasses.

"Hey, Zee," I said. "Can I have the usual, please?"

Zee gave a series of instructions to her apprentice, who selected the various muffins and cakes my family usually requested. After I'd paid, I said, "I wondered if I could have a word with your new assistant?"

"Sure," she said. "There's no problem, is there?"

I hope not. "Just need to clear something up."

Bag of goodies in hand, I waited for Carey to walk out from behind the counter. Like Zee, her clothes were covered in flour.

"Hey," said Carey. "You're Rory, right? From the library. I've seen your cousin around here a lot."

"Yeah," I said. "I hope you don't mind me asking you a couple of questions. You may have heard your ex-boyfriend ended up in a coma yesterday."

Her face fell. "Yeah. I heard he was found in the library. I guess it must have been tough for you to deal with."

Not the reaction I'd expected. "Someone spiked one of his fake arrows with a potion that put him to sleep, but until he wakes up, we're in the dark as to who did it. I've heard there are a lot of people who might have wanted him out of the way on Valentine's day."

"You might say that." She brushed flour off her apron. "He made a pretty bad name for himself."

"I'm told he was cruel to you after your breakup," I said.

"Cruel? More like annoying," she said. "I didn't like Ryan *that* much, but it was pretty vindictive of Harris to purposefully mess things up for us before we even got started. I just wanted someone to hang out with this Friday, so I didn't have to sit at home. It wasn't anything serious."

"Sorry," I said. "I'm hearing he made trouble for a lot of people, and since he was working for the library when it happened, we're trying to make sure it doesn't happen to the next person we hire. Do you know of anyone who might have had a particularly good reason to want to stop him?"

"He's a childish idiot," she said. "I'm glad I'm no longer wasting my time with him, but I don't care enough to want him out of a job. Anyone might have done it."

"Anyone who could have brewed up Poison Apple," I added. "I'm told that's not an easy potion to make, or to obtain."

"It's hard, but not impossible," she said. "Not if they knew someone who worked in the alchemy department on campus, for instance."

Oh, of course. "Is that likely?"

"One of the alchemy students might have been able to get their hands on the ingredients," said Carey. "Or they might even have asked another student to do it, if they were willing to risk being caught smuggling rare ingredients out of the labs. It wouldn't be the first time."

It'd slipped my mind that some of the students at the

university would have access to rare potion ingredients to use in their exams. If you took that into account, a lot more people would have had the means to brew up the potion. "Okay, thanks for talking to me."

I took the bag of muffins and cakes and walked back to the library, thinking hard. With no means to narrow down the pool of suspects, it was starting to look like we'd have to wait for Harris to wake up before we found out who was responsible for his current state, while crossing our fingers that the next person we hired didn't suffer the same fate.

Estelle's dismal expression brightened at the sight of my haul from the bakery. "I need a pick-me-up. The rumour mill is at it again. Half the students think there's a mysterious scorned lover going around shooting people with arrows. Never mind that Cupid was the one *carrying* the arrows to begin with."

I pulled a doughnut from the bag and bit into it, savouring the delicious taste of strawberry jam. "Have you had any luck finding a replacement?"

"Nope." She pulled a muffin out of the bag. "I thought I might ask some of the students if they might be interested, but they were grumbling about you throwing their beer out."

"It was that or have someone spill it on one of the books again," I said. "Anyway, I spoke to Roy James, who claims to be innocent of shooting Harris. He pointed me in the direction of Harris's ex, who works at the bakery, so I asked her a couple of questions while I was getting our supplies."

"His ex?" she echoed. "Would she have wanted to knock him out cold for a few days?"

"Maybe, but she put Roy back on the suspect list when she mentioned that the alchemy department at the university contains all the ingredients which would be needed to brew up the Poison Apple. Which means, theoretically, anyone might have 'borrowed' them."

Her shoulders slumped. "Oh. I didn't think of that."

"Then we'll go back to looking at the list of people who would have had a genuine reason to want Harris taken down," I said. "From the number of people he screwed over, it sounds like Harris caused most of the trouble himself. His ex told me he delivered a note to the guy she was seeing this weekend and caused him to call off their date."

"But you think she *didn't* do it?" Estelle bit into her muffin.

"She didn't strike me as guilty," I said. "Also, if she wanted to administer the potion, she could have just slipped it into his order from the bakery instead. Stealing one of his arrows and using it against him seems a bit too much hassle."

"That's a good point." Her brow crinkled. "The other arrows were fine, my mum said. It's like they wanted to send a message by making sure everyone saw he'd been stabbed by Cupid's arrow."

"The so-called Heartbreaker Killer," I said, thinking of the rumours Jet had picked up on. "It's got to be someone who went through a recent breakup. A bad one."

"Harris *caused* a fair few," said Estelle. "Besides, I don't think it would make the poetry night more popular if I walked up to the students and asked them to tell me all about their awful breakups."

"Fair enough," I said. "I do reckon it was supposed to be a statement of some kind. I just hope it's a one-off."

"You and me both." She glanced in the direction of our family's living quarters. "I hope Aunt Candace didn't get distracted while brewing the antidote."

"I'll go and check up on her. She's supposed to be giving me a magic lesson this afternoon, but it's anyone's guess as to whether she'll remember." I finished eating and made my way to the kitchen. There, Sylvester sat on the table, watching Aunt Candace levitate piles of ingredients into the cauldron boiling on the stove. The smell was even worse than before, not helped by the can of beer balanced on the side.

"You took the students' beer?" I said.

"I couldn't let it go to waste," answered Aunt Candace. "Come for your lesson, have you?"

"I thought you were busy with the antidote."

"I can multitask." She turned around to face me, her hair even wilder than usual thanks to the fumes from the potion. "This'll be good training for you."

"If I ever want to poison anyone?" I said. "What did Aunt Adelaide bribe you with?"

"None of your concern." She flicked a ladle at me, splattering the table with liquid. "My specialist skills are priceless. This particular antidote is trickier than an elf in a riddle contest and the ingredients are rarer than a publisher making a deadline."

"Okay…" I backed out of range in case she flicked more of the potion at me. "So what's our lesson about? Because that antidote's a bit beyond my level."

"You're so *rule-abiding*," she said, with a tutting noise. "Estelle is the same."

"I just have a highly developed sense of caution." With good reason. Misapplied magic could do a lot of damage.

"If that's the case…" She flicked her wand and a pile of roots flew over to the table. "I need someone to chop up those yarrow roots for me, and I don't have an extra pair of hands."

I frowned. "I thought we were supposed to be practising camouflage spells. Why not ask Sylvester to help?"

The owl hooted. "I have far more dignity. Also, I can't hold a knife."

I was starting to regret trying to hold Aunt Candace accountable at all, but at least helping her out would make it easier for me to learn the ingredients for the Poison Apple and its antidote.

After two hours of chopping, I was certain I'd never forget the smell of yarrow roots for as long as I lived. My eyes watered like I'd been chopping onions, dirt encrusted my nails, and the pile wasn't even half done.

Aunt Candace turned away from the pan, which was now emitting a green-yellow glow. "Fetch me some pixie wings, would you? I'm all out."

Grateful to escape the smell, I ran out the kitchen and headed to the cupboards in the living room where we kept our ingredient stores. I peered along rows of jars and picked out the one containing glittering wings.

Aunt Adelaide entered the living room as I closed the cupboard door. "Oh, hello, Rory. I wondered where you'd gone."

"I'm dealing with yarrow roots." I held the jar up. "Also, are these *actual* pixie wings?"

"Yes, they are," she said. "Don't tell me she made you chop the roots up yourself."

"Sylvester refused," I explained. "He's also been leading the students astray."

"I heard that!" the owl hooted from the kitchen. "I was merely trying to stop them from disturbing Estelle's balloons."

"The same balloons you nearly swept out the window?" I rolled my eyes, heading back to the kitchen behind my aunt.

"I thought I'd find you in here," Aunt Adelaide walked into the kitchen to address the owl. "Cass could have used your help upstairs. Someone left the door to the Magical Beings Division open."

I handed Aunt Candace the jar of wings. "Sylvester, are you even going to try helping us find the person who shot Harris? It wouldn't be hard for you to keep an eye out for trouble."

"If you want me to involve myself in gossip, that crow of yours can do it instead," he said, with a sniff. "I have already told you my thoughts on being used as a spy."

"You enjoy eavesdropping on *us*," I reminded him.

"Of course I do," he said. "You're much more interesting than the students' petty relationship drama."

"Might I remind you that Harris was shot on our own doorstep?" Aunt Adelaide said. "Go on, make yourself useful and give Cass a hand upstairs, Sylvester. Please."

"Well, all *right*." He took flight with an indignant hooting noise.

Aunt Candace had me chopping yarrow roots for another hour, before she stepped away from the stove.

"I am going to get ready for my date," she announced. "I shall need a long time to prepare."

"Want me to watch the potion?" I asked.

"You deserve a break." Aunt Adelaide re-entered the kitchen. "Candace, did you really need that many yarrow roots? You could have asked her to stop after the first batch."

I gave Aunt Candace an accusing look. "Seriously?"

"It's character-building." Aunt Candace left the kitchen, humming under her breath. "I'd use a strong cleaning spell to get rid of the smell of yarrow roots, or else that Reaper of yours might find himself otherwise engaged."

"I'm not seeing him tonight." I rose to my feet, abandoning the pile of roots. "Harris's mother hasn't come back yet, has she?"

"Not yet," said Aunt Adelaide grimly. "I'll watch the antidote while Candace is gone."

With some relief, I ran upstairs to shower, and to scrub off every trace of yarrow root from my skin.

When I got back downstairs, it was to find Aunt Candace sailing through the living quarters, dressed in a bright flowery number with mirrors dangling from the front and back.

"What in the world are you wearing?" asked Cass. "It looks like you fell through a greenhouse roof."

"Oi." She wagged a finger. "I'm going on my first date in a long while, and I intend to make an impression."

"A blind date doesn't mean you have to blind him with your own clothes," Cass said.

"Does your date know you're bringing your notebook?" I asked.

"It wouldn't be a blind date if he knew anything about me, now, would it?" She grinned. "And I know nothing about him, too. We're both blank pages, waiting to get to know one another."

"You don't know anything about him?" I said. "Not even his name?"

"I know he's supposed to be a vampire," she said. "That's it."

"Vampire?" said Estelle. "I thought you said you were swearing off vampires."

"I said no such thing." She drew herself upright in a clank of mirrors. "I will see you all later, where I will regale you with stories which will make your knees weak with jealousy."

Her mirrored dress clanked as she left the room, and I heard her clattering away through the lobby.

"At least her date will be able to hear her coming," I remarked. "I wish I'd asked Xavier to come to dinner with us today, while she's not here."

Though considering my hands still stank of yarrow roots, it was probably for the best that he stayed away.

4

Aunt Candace, who normally slept in later than the rest of us, was awake bright and early the following morning, humming away as she hovered over the cauldron on the stove. The rest of us gathered around the table for breakfast and tried to ignore the puffs of bright pink smoke emanating from the bubbling antidote.

"How was your date?" Aunt Adelaide asked.

"Interesting," Aunt Candace responded. "He wasn't a vampire after all, it turns out. It seems they got the names mixed up. The man I went out with was a werewolf. He had impeccable table manners, though."

Cass snorted. "What did he think of your notebook?"

"Funny thing, that," she said. "He didn't seem to notice it was there. He was too enamoured by my wit, I suppose."

Aunt Adelaide frowned. "Who doesn't know about your habit of taking notes on anyone you meet?"

"You'd be surprised," said Aunt Candace. "He seemed to think I was in charge of the library, which is hilarious, but I may have led him along a little… he didn't even ask about my books, which was a welcome relief, let me tell you."

Aunt Adelaide's expression froze. "Which werewolf was he, exactly? What was his name?"

"Peter Barley," said Aunt Candace, in dreamy tones. "Something wrong, sister?"

"I was told my date this Friday was supposed to be with a werewolf of that name," she said. "The pack's beta."

"Well, it's too late for that now," her sister replied. "We're seeing each other again on Friday. Did you know Hayley Sutton is hosting an event at the town hall?"

"You can't be serious," said Aunt Adelaide. "No wonder he didn't ask you about your books. He thought you were me."

Aunt Candace let out a cackle. "Now *that* is an interesting turn of events."

Aunt Adelaide's eyes narrowed. "That isn't funny, Candace. Did he even know *your* name?"

"Now you mention it… he never said," she said. "I assumed he did, but I wasn't paying too much attention at the time."

"No, I don't suppose you were," said her sister. "I'm supposed to have a date with him on Friday myself."

"Well, he's going to see me instead."

"That's deceptive," said Aunt Adelaide. "You can't run around pretending to be someone you aren't."

"Why not?" said Aunt Candace. "If this vampire is still expecting to meet me for a date, you're welcome to pretend to be me for the night. I'm sure it'll be very entertaining for everyone involved."

"Not at all," insisted Aunt Adelaide. "It's dishonest."

"You're too moral." Aunt Candace sniffed. "Live a little dangerously for once."

Aunt Adelaide muttered a curse under her breath. "I really hope you're working on that antidote, Candace."

"Yes, of course I am," she said. "Don't get your wand in a knot. Young Harris will be back on his feet in no time at all."

"I hope so." Estelle rose to her feet. "I still haven't found another Cupid."

Sensing my two aunts were about to kick off an argument, I got up and walked after Estelle into the library. "I can't believe Aunt Candace. You'd think the guy would have at least asked her name."

"He expected a woman with red hair. The two of them look enough like one another that he probably didn't realise there was anything amiss," said Estelle. "I hope Mum knows what she's doing, if she decides to go ahead with her own date and meet that vampire."

"It's not like she's going to pretend to be someone she's not, like Aunt Candace did," I said. "If they're both out on Friday night, that means I'm going to have to invite Xavier over tomorrow, assuming nobody kicks the bucket at the wrong moment."

Cass walked past the desk. "That's what you get for dating someone who deals with the dead for a living."

"Did you hear what Aunt Candace just said?"

She shrugged. "Something about the wrong date?"

"The blind dating service mixed the two of them up," I said. "So Aunt Candace got her sister's date, and she doesn't seem to have any intention of telling him who she really is."

"And Mum's dating... who?" said Cass.

"A vampire, assuming she goes ahead with it," said Estelle. "She'll probably call the blind dating service and explain the mix-up. I would. I mean, would you want your date to assume you're a totally different person to who they thought you'd be?"

"I thought that was the whole point," said Cass. "You're supposed to put on an act when you're on a first date, and then split up a week later when the truth comes out."

"Where'd you get that one from?" said Estelle. "That's terrible advice."

"And that is why I'm not in charge of this Valentine's day crap." Cass dumped a handful of glitter on the desk. "Speaking of crap, how did this end up in my bed?"

"Don't ask me," Estelle said to her retreating back. "Okay, I admit it, the glitter might have been a mistake."

"At least people won't forget us," I said. "If you ask me, you could do a better job of the blind dating service than Hayley Sutton."

"I can't even find a new Cupid," she said. "Zero applications. Nobody has shown the slightest bit of interest, not even the people on the reserve list."

"Maybe more people will see the ad when we open for the day," I said. "Why don't we make a bigger sign and hang it from the balconies so nobody can miss it?"

By the time the first patrons turned up for the day, it became clear that rumours of the so-called Heartbreaker Killer had swept across town, and the detail that Harris wasn't actually dead had somehow failed to make it into the story. The students walked in tight-knit groups as though expecting someone with a bow and arrow to take shots at them from the balconies and outright ignored the ad for a new Cupid.

By lunchtime, Estelle's mood was faltering. "I expected *one* person to express an interest," she said.

"Why don't we talk to the students ourselves?" I suggested. "We can reassure them their fears aren't legitimate—or if they are, we might get a clue as to who shot Harris."

"I guess that's our only option if we want to find someone new in time," said Estelle. "I'll finish returning these books, then I'll come and join you."

"Sure." I headed for the Reading Corner, glad not to see any stray beer cans this time around. The students remained huddled in groups, exchanging whispers and holding their wands close at hand as though they were afraid a ghostly Cupid would leap out from behind a shelf and start terrorising everyone.

"Hey," I said to the students at the nearest table. "Is anyone here interested in a part-time job delivering Valentine's cards this week? We pay well, and it can be arranged around your classes."

Several disinterested murmurs followed in answer.

"It's only for a few days," I went on. "You'll be well compensated for your time."

"Seems too risky," muttered a kid sitting on my left.

I turned to the speaker. "You aren't taking this whole Heartbreaker Killer thing seriously, are you? Harris isn't dead. It sounds like he annoyed a fair few people before he was shot, too, so if you aren't planning to deliver the wrong notes to the wrong people, you'll be fine."

Mutters broke out among the surrounding tables. I caught the words, "Nova wouldn't have needed an excuse."

"Excuse me?" I said. "Who's Nova?"

"Nova Lyle is an expert alchemist," said Roy James. "She and Harris had a major argument before the whole Cupid thing started. Next thing you know, he gets shot."

I turned to face Roy. "And you think she'd have been angry enough to shoot him with one of his own arrows?"

"She's a little eccentric," he replied. "Prone to overreacting. She threw a wart potion at me when I came into the lab without knocking while she was in the middle of an experiment. It took a week for me to get hold of a cure."

"Is she somewhere here in the library?" I asked.

"No," put in an Indian girl sitting at the table on my right. "Nova likes to work in total and utter silence. She's obsessive about it."

"Sounds like my aunt Candace," I said. "Speaking of whom, my aunt's working on the cure for Harris right now. In no time at all, he'll be back on his feet and he'll be able to tell us who shot him. I can pretty much guarantee the person who did it had a grudge against him in particular, not against Cupid or Valentine's Day in general."

"Exactly," said Estelle, stepping up beside me. "All you need is a good sense of fun and a willingness to wear a silly costume and get paid for it."

"Hey, Tyler is looking for work," said Roy James. "He quit working for Hayley Sutton and still has the costume, don't you?"

A dark-haired guy sitting at the back of the table startled. "What's that?"

"Are you interested in acting as our Cupid for the week?" asked Estelle.

Tyler's gaze darted to Roy with a hint of annoyance in

his expression, which smoothed out when he considered Estelle. "Would I only have to do it until Friday?"

"Monday," said Estelle. "We need Cupid to be at the poetry night, for the theme, you know."

"Well… all right," he said. "And I'd get paid then?"

"You bet," she said. "I'll throw in some extra benefits."

"In case I get shot with an arrow," he said. "I probably shouldn't joke about that, huh."

"Come with me," said Estelle. "We'll get your costume sorted."

Tyler obligingly followed us to the front desk. "Are you still trying to figure out who shot Harris?"

"I'm guessing the questions I was asking gave the game away," I said wryly. "We don't have any clear suspects. Do you know this Nova Lyle person? Apparently, she works in the lab all the time."

"She does," said Tyler. "Day and night."

"And she argued with Harris? Do you know why?"

"Probably because he disturbed her in the middle of brewing something tricky."

Even if this alchemist hadn't been responsible, she'd have had access to the ingredients to make the Poison Apple, or she might have seen who'd taken them out of the lab. The person who'd been responsible had either gone to an alchemist or got them from the labs on campus, and given the average budget of your typical student, I'd bet on the latter.

I'd looked for any admission of guilt among their faces, but I'd never been good at reading people. Books were much easier. Even the other students' reluctance to take on the job in Harris's place didn't necessarily mean any of them was guilty of shooting him. I mean, I'd be reluctant too, if I'd spent the past day hearing rumours that Harris had been shot dead by this so-called Heartbreaker Killer.

Estelle handed Tyler the bow and arrow he needed for his costume. "You'll start first thing tomorrow. I'll reopen the box so people can start leaving letters for you to deliver, and you should have plenty to start off with."

She put the cardboard box back on the front desk. At the moment, it was empty, save for a few sprinklings of glitter. Tyler shrugged the bag of arrows over his back and headed for the door, but before he could walk out, the door opened with a crash and Harris's mother strode into the library.

Uh-oh.

"Hello, Mrs Jones," I said in my most polite tones.

Her eyes narrowed. "Where is the antidote?"

"My aunt is working on it," I said. "The antidote will take several days to brew, as we told you."

She looked around with sharp eyes. "What are you all doing in here, then? Are you the one who replaced my boy? Thought you'd take his place, did you?"

Tyler shrank back away from her stare, looking alarmed. "No. I just wanted a job."

"Hang on," said Estelle. "I hired a replacement because we need someone who can step in before Saturday, and Harris won't wake up until after the antidote is brewed."

"How convenient." She gave a sniff.

Tyler, meanwhile, looked around as though debating the odds of making a run for the door before Mrs Jones caught him.

Estelle caught my eye and mouthed. *I'll deal with her.* I felt bad for leaving her behind, but if someone didn't get the new Cupid away, fast, at this rate we'd end up starting from scratch again.

Leaving Mrs Jones to voice her complaints, Cupid and I fled the library. When the door closed behind us, Tyler let out a low whistle. "Scary woman."

"Sorry about that," I said. "Not really how you wanted to start your new job, right?"

"No." He adjusted the arrows on his back. "I've had worse, though, and this isn't a bad way to make some quick cash."

"Did Roy say you used to work for Hayley Sutton?"

"I did," he confirmed. "I quit when two people got the wrong dates and kicked up a huge fuss."

"Sounds like that's a common scenario," I said. "I guess we're not the only hazardous working environment in town."

He finished adjusting his costume. "So… do you have a Valentine's card you want me to deliver?"

"Ah, no," I said. "I mean, the guy I'm dating knows I like him, and I don't know if Valentine's cards are his thing. Also, I doubt you want your first delivery to be to the graveyard."

"The grave… right, you're the one who's dating the Reaper." His eyes grew wide. "That's hardcore."

"Not really," I said. "He's quite laid-back, really. Has to be, considering his job."

His eyes widened even further. "Isn't he… a little scary?"

"No, of course not," I said. "I mean, when he gets his scythe out, I guess, but I wouldn't worry about that unless I was on my deathbed."

I guess that sounded kind of weird to anyone who

only knew of Xavier as the scary hooded Reaper who escorted souls into the afterlife. I didn't blame Tyler for looking at me as though he was seriously questioning my sanity.

I cleared my throat. "Since you're here, I don't suppose you'd mind showing me to the university campus? I think I'd like to talk to this Nova Lyle and find out if she saw anything odd at the lab."

5

Tyler led the way to the university campus on the far side of town, looking quite relieved to get away from the general vicinity of Mrs Jones. I didn't blame him a bit. I called Jet to fly alongside me in case I ran into trouble or got lost, since the streets over by the campus were unfamiliar to me.

The campus itself was fairly compact, consisting of a neat collection of brick buildings decorated with engravings indicating their department. Tyler pointed me to the alchemy department, which was decorated with stylised leaves and flowers. The strong smell of herbs emanated from the open windows.

Tyler halted at the door. "I should head off. You can find your way out, right? The lab Nova works in is behind the first door on the right."

"Sure." Even from the far side of town, the library was visible, towering over its neighbours. As long as I kept my eye on it, it was nearly impossible to get lost.

I opened the door, grimacing as the smell of herbs

turned to something more like sulphur mixed with garlic. On my right, a faded sign marked a door unambiguously titled 'Secret Lab'. Scrawled runes covered its battered wooden frame, which, I knew from working in the library, meant it was covered in protective wards to stop anyone from breaking inside.

There was a sudden loud boom. The door bounced in its frame and smoke seeped out of the edges, sending me jumping backwards out of range. Jet flew into the air with an exclamation of alarm, his wings flapping.

Coughing uncontrollably, I waited for the smoke to clear a little before rapping on the door with my knuckles. Jet flew around my head, making coughing noises.

"You should fly outside," I told him. "I'll come and join you later—I just want to make sure nobody's hurt in there."

I turned the door handle, but it didn't budge, not even when I pushed hard against it with my shoulder. Hoping I wasn't about to regret my decision, I pulled out my Biblio-Witch Inventory and tapped the word *unlock*. The door flew wide, and even more smoke billowed out from the room inside.

I blinked the sting of smoke from my eyes, as a young woman looked up from behind a smoking cauldron and scowled at me. Her frizzy black hair stood out at all angles, while her pale face was streaked with what appeared to be soot. "What are you doing in here?"

"Sorry," I choked. "Sorry to disturb you. I'm looking for Nova Lyle."

She gave a head-shake, then waved her wand. "Earplug charm. Didn't hear a word of that. Who are you?"

"Rory Hawthorn." I coughed again. "I heard the explosion and worried someone was hurt. I needed to talk to Nova Lyle."

"That's me," she said. "Relax, I'm just making a love potion."

"Was it supposed to explode?" Warily, I stepped into the room, but no more explosions greeted me.

"Not exactly, but love spells are tricky to brew," she said. "Who are you? I haven't seen you on campus before."

I closed the door behind me. "I work at the library."

Her jaw twitched with irritation. "What do you want here, then? Why'd you disturb me?"

"I don't know if you heard, but Harris Jones was recently put in a coma by someone who shot him with an arrow covered in Poison Apple."

She tilted her head. "That's even trickier to brew than a love potion. They must have been really mad at him."

"I figured," I said. "We think the person responsible might have obtained the ingredients from the labs here on campus. Since I'm told you spend a lot of time here, I wondered if you might have noticed anything."

"I didn't see anyone brewing it," she said. "But I'm one of only a few people who use this room. Nobody else wants to come in at the same time as me, for some reason."

I can't imagine why. I found myself fervently glad that Aunt Candace's need for her own space generally didn't involve blowing things up. "Have you seen anyone removing a large number of rare ingredients recently? Someone who wouldn't have any reason to?"

"I don't keep track," she said. "I'm working on this new project and it's taking up all my free time."

"All right," I said. "Is there anyone you know of who

might have reason to target Harris Jones, then? I'm told he made enemies everywhere. I'm also told you were one of them."

"Enemies?" She wrinkled her nose. "I wouldn't say that. I haven't spoken to the guy since he knocked over three of my expensive vials the other week."

"So that's why you argued?"

"Yeah, but I wouldn't waste my best ingredients on him," she said. "Ask his ex-girlfriend. She might know. I don't get involved in that sort of thing. I'm not interested in dating anyone."

"I already spoke to her." I scanned the floor for any signs of the bright potion which had covered the arrow, but given the state of the room, it was beyond me to tell if any vials of deadly sleeping potions were hidden anywhere. I wasn't enough of an expert at potion-making to be able to tell one from another. It didn't help that the whole room smelled of whatever had exploded, as well as that pungent garlic-and-sulphur combination which made even the yarrow roots look tame by comparison. "Thanks for your time. Can you come to the library and let us know if you remember anything else?"

"Sure." She tipped a vial over the cauldron, and I hastily closed the door as another muffled explosion shook the room.

———

"No luck?" Estelle looked up from the desk as I entered the library, pausing to use a cleaning spell on my shoes to get rid of the debris from the lab.

"Nope," I said. "Nova Lyle works while wearing an

earplug charm strong enough to block out the apocalypse and doesn't watch the cupboards. But she says people go in and out of there all the time and nothing stood out to her as suspicious in the last week. How was Mrs Jones?"

"Sylvester of all people had to intervene in the end." She grinned. "It was almost worth knowing she'll be saying horrible things about us behind our backs to see him chasing her out of here, hooting like a maniac."

"I should have stuck around to watch," I said. "I know I had to get Tyler out of there, but it wasn't fair that you had to handle Mrs Jones yelling at you."

"Better than losing another Cupid," she said. "Anyway, I'm the one who hired him, so it's all on me."

"We couldn't have predicted Cupid's mother would turn out to be a terrifying control freak," I said. "Has she got the message that we're going as fast as we can?"

"She's got the message that we have an angry owl on security duty," said Estelle. "But the antidote depends on Aunt Candace staying on track, and she's totally lost in her head at the moment. More than usual, if possible."

"Then we'll send someone to supervise her," I said. "Nova—the girl who works in the lab—seemed to think Harris was shot as a result of a personal grudge, nothing more. Now we have another Cupid, there's nothing to stop the rest of the week from going ahead without any issues."

"I hope you're right," she said. "Want a movie night after we're done for the day? I think we've earned it."

"That sounds perfect."

———

The following morning brought a new spate of letters for Cupid to deliver. The town's citizens seemed to have got over their cold feet now we had a brand-new Cupid on the team. I volunteered to work on the front desk to make up for my absence yesterday—while crossing my fingers that Mrs Jones didn't show her face this time—so Estelle would have time to put the new Cupid through his paces.

After a lull in visitors, a huge man walked into the library who didn't look like he belonged among the usual crowd in the slightest. Tall, blond, and muscled like a lumberjack, he looked like he'd be more at home running through a field or lifting something heavy than browsing through the stacks.

"Can I help you with something?" I called out.

"Is your aunt around today?" asked the man.

"Which one?" I said. "Aunt Candace is brewing up a potion and Aunt Adelaide is in the back."

"Adelaide," he said. "I've been having trouble reaching her on the phone."

A faint cackling noise came from over my shoulder. I looked around and spotted Sylvester perched on the bookshelf immediately behind the front desk.

"There you are," I said to him. "Will you fetch Aunt Adelaide?"

"Are you *quite* sure that's who you want me to fetch?" said the owl. "What did you say your name was?"

"Peter," said the blond newcomer. "Is there a problem?"

Peter. Wait a minute. He must be the werewolf Aunt Candace had gone on a date with, and he thought she was Aunt Adelaide. Clearly, she still hadn't enlightened him on the truth.

I cleared my throat. "Sorry, there's been a misunder-standing—"

"I will fetch her." Sylvester took flight in a loud beat of wings, soaring so close to my head that he forced me to duck behind the desk to avoid being clawed.

"Does that bird work here in the library?" asked the werewolf.

"He's our assistant." I straightened upright. "You went on a date with my aunt, right?"

"I had a fantastic time with her the other day," he said. "She's a remarkable woman. It's incredible how she's managed to run the library single-handedly for all this time, as well as raising you children."

"Ah—I'm not hers," I said clumsily. "I mean, I'm Estelle and Cass's cousin, Rory. I moved here a couple of months ago."

"Oh, the lost cousin," he said. "That's what they call you, right?"

"Yes," I said, wishing I could drag Aunt Candace out to have this conversation herself instead of me. "Have you ever noticed she's not *quite* the same as the description in her profile?"

"Oh, I didn't read any profile of hers before our date," he said. "The blind dating service doesn't encourage it. I only had her name—though everyone knows the library, of course. I wondered if she'd be interested in going to the party at the town hall this Friday."

"Um." *Why, Aunt Candace?* "I'm not sure she's into that kind of thing."

Luckily—or perhaps not—the woman herself sailed into the lobby at that moment, sparing me from having to prolong our conversation.

"Oh, hello, Peter," Aunt Candace said.

"Hello, Adelaide," said Peter. "I see why the library has hosted hundreds of events. You're right—it has a wonderful atmosphere."

I was pretty sure Aunt Candace had never called the library 'wonderful' in her life.

"Speaking of parties," I said to Aunt Candace, "I thought you hated them—"

"I'll give you a tour of the library later," Aunt Candace interrupted me, addressing the werewolf. "Want to go for a walk? I hardly get outside these days."

More like she didn't want to risk running into Aunt Adelaide and giving the game away. "You don't, because you're always in your writing—"

Sylvester hooted at full volume, drowning out my words. Aunt Candace seized the opportunity to take the werewolf's arm and steer him out of the library.

I shook my head after her. "She is unbelievable."

"I find it perfectly believable," said the owl.

"And just why are you playing along with this ridiculous game?" I asked the owl.

Sylvester flew down onto the desk. "It amuses me."

"I bet it does," I said. "I suppose at least they're double-dating *outside* the library, so the rest of us don't have to watch. Where's Aunt Adelaide? The real one, I mean. Aren't you going to tell her?"

"I'm not a snitch." Sylvester took flight and disappeared in a flutter of wings.

"Seriously?" Knowing Sylvester, he planned to drop the truth bomb at the worst possible time. For instance, during tonight's family dinner. With Xavier. *Oh, god.*

I was on the brink of heading off to find Aunt Adelaide

myself before she learned what her sister was up to, but an instant later, the door flew open again. The new Cupid ran into the library and slammed the door behind him, breathing hard. His wings hung off his shoulders, dripping wet, and he left a damp trail of footsteps behind him.

"What happened to you?" Had someone attacked him?

"Morris Wilson chased me down and used a firebomb spell on me," he said. "Apparently, the last Cupid caused a breakup between him and his girlfriend because she found out about his crush on some Maura person. Supposedly, it's *my* fault for delivering a letter to his girlfriend that was addressed to Maura. Which I didn't, because I wasn't here."

My heart sank. "He should have known you and Harris weren't the same person. Didn't he check?"

"I don't think he cared," he said. "He saw the costume and went straight for his wand. I had to jump into the sea to put out the flames."

That explained the state of his costume. He shrugged the wings off, where they fell into a damp, smoking heap on the carpet.

Estelle emerged from a side door and hurried over. "What happened?"

"Morris Wilson happened," he said, morosely. "Firebomb spell. I panicked and ran for the nearest water source. Sorry about the carpet."

"No worries." Estelle flicked her wand, and his costume—and the carpet—dried in an instant. "Morris Wilson? Why did he target you?"

"He had an issue with the last Cupid." He scooped up the wings in his arms. "You know, I'm not sure I'm cut out for this job after all."

"I'll have a word with him," said Estelle. "Morris, I mean. Where did you see him?"

"On the high street," he said. "He came out of the apothecary and ran at me. I don't think he'll have gone far."

"And what does he look like?" I asked.

"He's really tall," said Cupid. "He's wearing a green cloak. Bright green. Looks like a Christmas tree. He's easy to spot."

"We'll find him," said Estelle. "Right, Rory?"

"Who's going to watch the desk?" I looked for Sylvester, but the traitorous owl had disappeared. "Jet?"

The little crow flew down to land on my shoulder. "Yes, partner?"

"Can you fetch Aunt Adelaide or Cass and ask them to watch the desk? Estelle and I are heading out for a few minutes."

"Of course, partner!" squeaked Jet, launching into flight.

"I doubt Cass will be pleased at being dragged downstairs," Estelle said, pushing the library door open.

"Where's Aunt Adelaide, do you know?" I walked out behind her, glancing behind me at the lobby.

"Watching Aunt Candace's antidote," she said. "Since she's not around."

"No, she's gone on a nice walk with a werewolf while pretending to be your mother."

Estelle's mouth dropped open. "Is she with Peter Barley right now?"

"Yes," I said. "Sylvester thought it was funny to stop me from giving the game away, so he's still under the impression he's dating your mum."

"What *is* Aunt Candace playing at?" she said. "She should have told him the truth as soon as she realised the mix-up."

I walked with her across the town square in the direction of the high street. "I guess she's banking on the rest of us being distracted. Which we are. How can anyone have mistaken Tyler for Harris?"

Estelle tucked a strand of red hair behind her ear. 'I forgot some people would see the costume and jump to conclusions. Maybe I should have thrown out the whole plan."

"Most people aren't that short-sighted." I understood her concern, though. If we lost two Cupids within the space of a week, at this rate we'd have nobody to stand in during the Valentine's-themed poetry night on Monday.

As for Aunt Candace, the werewolf seemed to genuinely like her, but how much of her behaviour had been acting and how much had been the real her? This was her mess to resolve, whatever the case, so I put it out of mind and focused on keeping an eye out for any signs of the guy who'd attacked Tyler.

We headed down the winding high street, where my gaze landed on a man who must have been a good six and a half feet tall, wearing a vivid green cloak. Estelle zeroed in on him, too. "Accurate description, right?"

"Yeah, tell me about it." I sidestepped a group of shoppers laden with bags. There must be some kind of sale on pointed hats, because some of the shoppers wore up to a dozen hats balanced on their own heads. Even so, the green-cloaked wizard stood taller than most of them.

"Hey," Estelle called out. "You're Morris Wilson, right?"

The green-cloaked wizard wheeled around on the spot. "Who wants to know?"

"We do." Estelle halted behind him. "You just threw a firebomb spell at my employee for doing his job."

He blinked. "You mean Harris? I didn't know he worked for you."

"Harris is already in a coma because someone shot him with one of his own arrows laced with a sleeping potion," said Estelle. "Tyler is my new employee, and he only started on the Cupid job today. He can't possibly have done anything to warrant you using an offensive spell."

"Oh." A sheepish look came over him. "I didn't see his face. I just saw the wings."

"Well, don't do it again," Estelle said. "Whatever Harris did to you—"

"He broke my girlfriend's heart," he said.

"Oh?" I said. "What exactly do you mean by that?"

"Like I said," he said tersely. "He thought it was funny to tell her I was crushing on Maura Tansey."

"Not that it's any of my business, but that's no reason to shoot the messenger," said Estelle.

"What, you think I put the guy in a coma?" he said.

"You did just firebomb-spell our new Cupid," I reminded him. "You know that's illegal, right?"

"So is using magic to mess with people's love lives," he said stubbornly. "Which is what Harris was doing."

"Magic?" I frowned. "What do you mean, magic?"

"How many breakups has the guy caused in the last week?" he said. "Either he has a knack for bad timing, or he's doing it purpose."

"So you're claiming you *don't* have a crush on Maura?" said Estelle. "If Harris was only doing what you asked him to do in the first place, then you can hardly blame him for delivering a letter you wrote yourself."

"That's just it—I *didn't* write a letter to Maura," he said. "He found out about my crush on her, who knows how, and delivered my girlfriend a letter addressed to her that was supposed to be from me."

"You didn't write it?" I said. "Are you sure?"

"Of course I'm sure," he said. "I think I'd remember deliberately sabotaging my own relationship."

"So you think Harris wrote the note himself?" I asked.

"Just ask him," he said. "Oh, right, he's in a coma. How… I mean, how likely is he to wake up?"

"He should wake up within a few days, when the antidote is ready," I said. "As for proof, does your ex still have the note? Is it your handwriting?"

"She said it is, but I haven't seen it myself," he said. "It was enough to convince her, anyway."

"If you really think Harris wrote it himself, magic or no magic, we could use a look at it," said Estelle. "He might have done the same to others, too."

That, or Morris was lying, but it seemed a bizarre story to make up, especially if it hadn't saved his relationship in the end.

"I reckon it's too late for Liz and me," he said. "But if you want to find out, I can take you to speak to her."

6

Estelle and I walked behind Morris as he continued on his path up the high street. I didn't believe for a minute he was innocent of any wrongdoing, but it was possible there'd been a genuine misunderstanding when he'd targeted Tyler with a fire-bomb spell. Or he needed glasses.

"It sounds like Harris was really trying to hurt people," I remarked. "Finding out people's secret crushes and then using that information to wreak havoc."

"Maybe," said Estelle. "But if he delivered a note supposedly written by Morris to his girlfriend, it must have been convincing enough for her."

"True." It was possible Morris was making the whole story up, but when you added up all the people Harris had ticked off, it was clear there was something amiss. The question was, if Morris really hadn't written the note, how had Harris found out about his supposed crush?

Morris led us up to the west side of campus, where a number of brick buildings housed the student accommodation. He walked up to one of the apartment blocks and rang the buzzer. "Fair warning—she won't be happy to see me again."

I stepped back as the door opened, revealing a young woman with warm brown skin and braided hair. Her eyes narrowed at the sight of our companion.

"You," she said. "You lying, cheating—"

"I didn't cheat," he insisted. "It was a misunderstanding."

"You 'accidentally' wrote a letter telling Maura that you like her, and then you tried to deny you wrote the damned thing when Cupid delivered it to me instead of her?"

"I didn't—" He broke off. "I mean, can I see the letter?"

Her mouth trembled. "I gave it to the person it was addressed to. I wasn't going to *keep* it."

"Where is Maura, then?" he said.

"Find her yourself." Her sharp gaze found Estelle and me. "Who are they? Didn't you have the guts to come here alone?"

"Ah, we're from the library," Estelle said. "We're here because it seems the person we employed to act as Cupid may have been delivering fake letters to people in an effort to sabotage their relationships."

"The letter sure looked real to me." She sniffed. "I can't believe you were so terrified to admit to the truth that you dragged strangers into our business, Morris. We're through."

She slammed the door tightly behind her, causing Morris to jump violently backwards. "It's not a cover story! Someone framed me."

"Did you write the letter or didn't you?" Estelle said.

"Because if you're lying to us, it's going to take even longer for us to find who was responsible for shooting Harris."

He winced. "I don't remember writing to Maura. Yeah, I liked her, but it wasn't worth screwing up what I had with Liz."

"Maura has the letter, though, she said," I said to him. "Where is she at the moment?"

"I don't know. The communal learning area, maybe." He turned away from the block, his face flushed. "I swear I didn't mean for anyone to find out. It's possible I might have let something slip while I was drunk, but I think I'd remember writing a letter and posting it to her."

"And bringing it to the library," I added. "Do you remember posting a letter in Cupid's box?"

"No," he said. "I don't."

Estelle and I exchanged bewildered glances. Either he was a better actor than he seemed, had an abysmal memory, or some level of trickery had been involved. Or magic. *Hmm.*

"Then we'll see Maura ourselves," I said. "Assuming she won't get mad at you, too."

"No… she thought it was funny when she found out." He sighed. "I screwed up both relationships at once."

"So you *were* thinking of cheating?" said Estelle.

"No!" he said. "I would never. I don't know what came over me."

Suppose he was telling the truth, and Harris had orchestrated the whole thing? I hadn't picked up any weird vibes from him in the time he'd worked at Cupid, but in truth, I hadn't been paying close attention to the people who asked him to deliver notes. As for whether

Morris had been to the library recently, it would be easy enough to verify if we asked the other students.

Morris walked ahead of us, his head down. It was easier to blame him for his own misfortune, but perhaps there was something more going on. Until we saw the letter, we could only guess.

Morris used a key card to unlock the way into the communal learning area, which covered the ground floor of a modern building with transparent walls. Half of it was set aside for practising spells, while the rest was covered in tables where students worked in groups or alone. Morris approached a young red-haired woman with glasses, who sat alone at a table, typing on her laptop.

The woman raised an eyebrow when she spotted Morris. "Can I help you?"

"I wanted—" He swallowed. "Liz told me she gave you the letter. The letter Cupid delivered to her, I mean."

"I thought I was the one you wanted him to give the letter to." A flicker of amusement stirred in her eyes. "I read it. It was sweet."

"I don't—" He broke off. "I think there's been a misunderstanding. I mean, Liz and I... we weren't supposed to break up over it."

The amusement faded from her face. "Look, I'm flattered, but if you don't have the guts to face up to what you did to Liz, I'm not getting involved."

"But do you have the note?" he pressed.

She frowned at Estelle and me. "Why are you two here? Did he recruit you to back him up?"

"We're here investigating an attack on the student we hired as our Cupid," I explained. "You might have heard

Harris was put into a coma a few days ago, so we're talking to everyone he delivered letters to."

"Well, why didn't you say so?" She reached into her bag and pulled out a crumpled note. "It's your handwriting, Liz said. I should have thrown it out, but whatever."

Morris took the note from her. For a moment, he just stared at it. Then he turned and walked away, towards the exit. Estelle and I followed behind him, catching him up at the doors.

"What is it?" asked Estelle.

"It's my handwriting," he mumbled. "I swear I don't remember writing it *or* posting it in Cupid's box. I haven't even been to the library this week."

"If you didn't post it, how did Cupid get hold of it, then?" I asked.

"I didn't *write* it, let alone post it." He groaned and shoved the note into his bag. "I also don't know what I saw in Maura, come to that."

"She had a point about you acting like a coward," said Estelle. "Sort things out with your ex first. That's the best way to get out of this situation."

"I guess you're right," he said. "Besides, I don't have any other options now."

Leaving him to it, Estelle and I made our way out of the campus and back towards the library.

"Is it possible he was telling the truth?" I asked Estelle. "I mean, it's more likely he was lying to save face because he's embarrassed that he got caught, but I assume it's possible to fake someone's handwriting using magic."

"It is," she confirmed. "There are strict rules for examinations for that very reason, but the university wouldn't reinforce them for something as mundane as writing

Valentine's cards. To be honest, I don't know what to believe. He *was* acting like a coward. Writing a card to someone he had a crush on and making Cupid deliver it on his behalf? If he'd handed it directly to her, he wouldn't have got caught."

"Yeah, it sounds like excuse-making to me," I said. "Still, I don't think Harris was entirely innocent in this. He knew both of them, so he must have known the impact of delivering the note to Morris's girlfriend instead of Maura."

"Yeah, I can see that," said Estelle. "We need to talk to the other students who felt wronged by him to see if there's any other signs he might have manipulated the situation, but that'll take forever."

"Don't worry about it," I said. "You should focus on planning the rest of the Valentine's events, and I'll focus on stopping our new Cupid from getting hit by any more hostile spells. Maybe I should assign Sylvester to act as his bodyguard as a punishment for playing along with Aunt Candace's games."

A reluctant smile stirred on her face, swiftly disappearing. "I still think I should have noticed if something was off with Harris," she said. "I'm the one who hired him."

"You couldn't tail him around while he was delivering the letters, could you?" I said. "You'd think he'd want the money too badly to screw it up on purpose. That, and he didn't care about potential retaliation."

It seemed weird for him to take a part-time job as Cupid and then use it to spread discord and anger, too. So much about the situation made no sense, but considering Harris remained comatose, it wasn't possible for us to do any more than play a guessing game and hope nobody else mistook the new Cupid for him.

"I guess not," she said. "Some people just want to cause chaos for no apparent reason. I mean, look at Aunt Candace."

"Or for research," I added. "Which is pretty much the same thing with her. Do you want to tell your mum she's out pretending to be her, or should I?"

She groaned. "Do you want things to be really awkward at dinner when Xavier shows up?"

"Things will be awkward whether she finds out now or later," I pointed out. "Maybe I should have invited him to come another time."

"When our family *isn't* mired in drama?" she said. "Are things ever normal in the library?"

"Fair point." I spotted a group of students crossing the square. "There, you can ask them if they saw Morris going into the library to leave a card for Cupid to deliver. It's worth a shot."

We approached the group, which included Roy Jones and several of the others who'd been in the library earlier.

"Hey," Estelle said to them. "I hope you don't mind, but I wanted to ask you a question."

"Is it about whoever just attacked your new Cupid?" Roy said. "Because it wasn't us."

"No, it was a guy called Morris Wilson," said Estelle. "Do you know him?"

"Not well," said Roy. "Why?"

"He made some odd claims about Harris," I said. "Have you seen Morris in the library at all over the last couple of weeks?"

"The library?" echoed Roy. "I haven't, but I wasn't paying attention. You think he attacked Cupid?"

"He claims someone planted a letter in Cupid's delivery box that he never wrote," said Estelle. "Since the letter in question was addressed to someone else, they both got mad at him."

"Sounds like what happened with you and Darcey," Roy nudged a girl with red hair, who flushed.

Estelle turned to her with a kind smile. "What happened? If you don't mind sharing."

"I wrote a letter to a girl I have a crush on," she mumbled. "But I didn't post it. I just wrote it and put it away because I was too scared to give it to her. Then… a couple of days later, she sent me a message telling me Cupid delivered the note to her. I was sure there was a mistake, but I searched my whole room for the note and couldn't find it. I would remember if I'd posted it in Cupid's box."

"Someone took it out of your bag and posted it?" I said, nonplussed.

"Harris is in three of my classes," she said. "So he had more than one opportunity to. Can't say I know why he'd bother, though."

"Yeah, that is weird," I said. "How'd it turn out?"

"Good." Her expression brightened. "Turns out she likes me, too, so we're going to the event at the town hall tomorrow night. But it might just as easily have turned out badly."

"No kidding." I was even more perplexed now. "Did he see you writing the note, or overhear you talking to anyone else about liking her?"

"Maybe," she said. "I just didn't expect it."

"Sounds like you needed the push," Estelle said kindly. "But if you hear any stories about anyone who had a less than positive outcome from Harris's actions, can you point them in my direction?"

"Sure thing," said the girl.

Feeling even more baffled than before, we entered the library to find Cass sitting at the front desk, her head buried in a book. One of Aunt Candace's, by the look of things. She'd stopped hiding her liking for our aunt's books when it had sunk in that we wouldn't tease her for it.

"Where's Cupid?" I asked.

"Went home," said Cass, without looking up. "He did all the deliveries."

"He did?" Estelle peered into the box on the desk. "Are you sure there aren't any letters back there that might have fallen out of the box?"

Cass raised her head. "You can't blame people for not wanting to end up with their dirty secrets aired in public."

"I didn't think you were even paying attention," said Estelle. "We just went to talk to Morris, the guy who attacked Cupid. Seems Harris thought it was funny to give his girlfriend a note meant for another woman. Needless to say, she wasn't amused."

"Am I supposed to care?" said Cass.

"He claims he never wrote the note to begin with." I said. "We just heard about another incident where some-one's note was delivered to the intended recipient when they never posted it in the box. It's possible Harris was eavesdropping on people."

"And snatching notes from people's private notepads," added Estelle.

"Remind me why we're brewing up an antidote for this guy again?" said Cass.

"Because he was injured on the job," said Estelle. "And we might be the only people who can."

Or the only people who will, at this rate.

But with him in a coma, the odds of us finding the truth before he woke seemed as slim as the odds of Aunt Candace having a change of heart and coming clean to Peter the werewolf.

————

Estelle was still in an uncharacteristically grim mood by the time Xavier arrived that evening. Aunt Candace had yet to return from her 'walk' with Peter, while Aunt Adelaide had remained hunched over the antidote in the kitchen for so long that I worried telling her the truth about her sister's antics would cause her to flip out and hex her.

It was too late to cancel tonight's date, so I went to meet Xavier at seven. He arrived promptly, and I opened the door the instant I heard a knock. "Hey."

"Hey." He pulled me close and kissed me, and I let the day's worries fall off my shoulders. "Great to see you."

"Are you two going to stand there cuddling all day or are you going to let me in?" said Aunt Candace's voice from somewhere in the gloom outside.

I released Xavier, and my aunt reached the steps, her hair windswept and a ridiculous smile on her face. "I thought you weren't coming back at all."

"Don't be absurd." She sidled into the library. "I wouldn't miss dinner with the Reaper for the world."

"Then I hope you'll be on your best behaviour," I told her. "Your sister isn't thrilled with you for leaving her in charge of the antidote all day."

"It won't kill her." Aunt Candace skipped through the lobby, humming a little tune.

I turned to Xavier and grimaced. "Last chance to back out."

He trailed a hand though my hair. "I reckon I can take it."

Bracing myself, I stepped over the threshold and into the lobby, which was lit up for the evening with lanterns floating along the balconied edges of the upper levels. Aunt Candace skipped ahead through the narrow corridor on the left-hand side and into the dining room.

Aunt Adelaide, who was levitating plates onto the table, shot a scowl at Aunt Candace but didn't offer a comment. Cass and Estelle already sat at the table, the former with her head in the same book she'd been reading earlier. Estelle looked up and smiled. "Hey, Xavier."

Cass gave a brief glance at him and then returned to her book.

"Oh, hello," said Aunt Adelaide. "I'm afraid we're running a little late. I've been busy brewing an antidote today, as Rory may have told you. It was supposed to be a shared job, but some of us had other plans."

Aunt Candace ignored the jab and took a seat at the table. She wore a flowery dress—thankfully without any mirrors this time—and her tangled hair gave her the overall appearance of a redheaded scarecrow. "Go on, take a seat. Our guest should sit at the head of the table, of course."

Xavier sat. "I'm glad to be here."

Cass made a faint noise of scepticism, stifled when her mother gave her a stern look as she sat beside her sister. That left me to sit on the other end of the table, with my whole family between me and Xavier. Suddenly, I didn't have much of an appetite, but the quicker this was over with, the better. I sat down and poked at my food with a fork.

Aunt Candace studied me, then Xavier. "I heard Reapers didn't need to eat," she said.

Xavier looked up. "We don't need to, but I do miss the local ice cream."

"They say it's to die for," said Aunt Candace. "I suppose you'd know."

I shot her a warning look. "Xavier isn't dead."

"No, he's taking a temporary trip to an unearthly plane," said Aunt Candace. "That's what I gathered, based on my reading. It's remarkable what you can glean by reading the right books, know what I mean?"

I glared at her, but Aunt Candace seemed undeterred. She was riding the high of her day with Peter the were-wolf, which made her even more insufferable than usual. I found myself glad of Aunt Adelaide's cooking, which shut her up for a few minutes. I, meanwhile, began a mental countdown to the end of the meal, when I'd make an excuse for Xavier and me to go for a walk outside.

"So," said Aunt Candace, after a lengthy pause. "What's it like working for the angel of death?"

"Rather like any customer service job, I imagine," Xavier said. "The deceased often argue with me about whether it's their time to go or not. They seem to think they know better than the Reaper does."

"Even with dead people, the customer is always right,"

said Aunt Candace. Her notebook and pen floated under the table, but since she hadn't started asking any dangerous questions yet, I let it slide. If she wanted to risk the Grim Reaper's wrath by mentioning his secrets in her books, I wouldn't be able to stop her.

"You'd think it would be hard to argue when your body's lying dead on the ground," he added. "Not that they don't try anyway. Denial is a powerful thing."

"Yes," said Cass, with a significant look at me. "It is."

What's she getting at this time? I averted my gaze and focused on Xavier instead. "I guess good manners are hard to come by, even in death."

"Do you sleep in a coffin?" Aunt Candace asked him.

"Nah, that's vampires," I said. "Reapers don't need to sleep."

"So they don't." Aunt Candace's eyes glinted, and she wore a knowing smirk which suggested she'd already known. "I'm assuming he still has a bed for... other activities."

My face went scarlet. "Aunt Candace."

"Just curious," she said brightly. "For research purposes, you understand. It's essential to have an understanding of these things."

"No, it isn't," I said irrationally, my face somewhere between tomato red and the surface of the sun.

"You did remember to turn off the stove, didn't you, Candace?" Aunt Adelaide interrupted. "If you didn't, the antidote will be ruined."

Alarmed, I forgot all about Aunt Candace's comment. "Seriously?"

"I'll save it." Aunt Candace swooped to her feet and out of the room, her dress flying behind her like a cape.

Aunt Adelaide followed her sister, leaving me with my cousins and Xavier. This was going even worse than planned and the subject of Aunt Candace's latest subterfuge hadn't even come up. I had the sneaking suspicion Aunt Adelaide had fabricated the antidote issue on purpose, and if I had any sense, I'd get Xavier out of here before they came back.

"Antidote?" asked Xavier.

"For the Poison Apple," I told him. "I did say to ignore everything Aunt Candace says, right?"

"I didn't forget." He shot me a grin. "This is a lot more entertaining than an evening with the Grim Reaper."

Cass looked up, an uncharacteristic smile on her face. "Has the Grim Reaper ever fornicated with mortals?"

My embarrassment turned to horror. "I doubt anyone's ever lived long enough to ask."

"You aren't wrong," said Xavier, no longer sounding amused. "The Grim Reaper isn't a human. The rest is classified."

"Ooh." Aunt Candace was back. "What's classified?"

I gave Cass a pleading look, which she returned with a smirk. "Whether the Reaper can procreate with humans."

I wished I could sink through the floor into the vampire's basement, but no such luck. Xavier didn't seem embarrassed, just annoyed, with good reason. Reaper secrets were serious business.

"You're welcome to ask him yourself," Xavier said. "If you don't mind your time to leave being moved up a little."

"What's his problem with humans knowing about Reapers, anyway?" Cass said. "Is it really that dire if a human knows whether the Grim Reaper can sleep with one of them or not? It's not *that* important to the Reaping business, surely."

"Unless it runs in the family," said Aunt Candace. "Is he your father? The Grim Reaper?"

The expression on Xavier's face froze. "Excuse me?"

"Candace!" Aunt Adelaide snapped. "That's enough."

"Aren't you curious, though?" her sister pressed. "Most people haven't seen the Grim Reaper in the flesh, let alone without that cloak… but Rory saw him without his hood on. I heard he had the most stunning blue eyes."

Never mind the vampire's basement—I wouldn't have minded taking up residence in the earth's core. "You can't be crushing on the Grim Reaper. You're dating that werewolf dude, besides, assuming he doesn't find out who you really are."

Aunt Adelaide gave her sister a sharp look. "You're *still* deceiving him?"

Xavier cleared his throat. "I think I should leave."

"Wait." I jumped to my feet. "Please don't feel pressured to leave."

"There's no need to look at me like that," said Aunt Candace to her sister. "Peter is much better suited for me than for you."

"I'm not surprised, if he thinks you *are* me," Aunt Adelaide responded.

Xavier glided out of the room, and I hastened to follow him.

"I'm sorry," I said. "Aunt Candace is in a bizarre mood today, as you can probably tell, but we can always go for a walk instead. Honestly, I'd prefer it."

A crash sounded from the kitchen, and I winced. *Please tell me that wasn't the antidote.*

Xavier halted in front of the doors. "I think you should probably help your family, Rory. It sounds like they need a voice of reason in there."

No kidding. "We can do this again another time when everything calms down."

"Sure." He gave me a faint smile. "I'll see you later."

I opened my mouth to apologise again, but he was already walking through the doors and out into the night.

I found Estelle hiding in the kitchen, watching the antidote, while my aunts continued to bicker in the dining room.

"You're being ridiculous!" Aunt Candace was saying.

Aunt Adelaide's voice rose louder. "You do realise Peter is the beta of the local werewolf pack, don't you? Do you want us to make enemies of the entire pack?"

"We won't be enemies," said Aunt Candace. "He likes me."

"He has no idea who you really are." I walked back into the dining room. "And to be honest, I don't, either. What the hell was that in aid of? Were you *trying* to drive Xavier off?"

"I assumed he came prepared for questions," said Aunt Candace. "How many times will I get to ask the Reaper about his job?"

"A lot more if you don't pressure him into getting out his scythe and using it on you," I said. "And you, too, Cass. You're not researching a book, so you had no reason to ask stupid questions."

Cass slammed her book closed. "I was trying to do you a favour," she said. "I assume you haven't slept with him, but if the question ever comes up, you'll want to know if it's possible, right?"

I gaped at her. "You were so concerned for my love life that you decided to ask him personal questions in front of everyone without my permission? Rather than, say, letting me ask him myself?"

"Well, you two are always doing your own thing, so I haven't had the chance to," she said. "Also, it sounds like you *haven't* asked him a lot of important questions. Like why you can see into Death."

I backed up into the doorway. "How on earth do you know that?"

"You talked about it before," she said. "I assume it isn't a big secret."

"You assumed wrong." Aunt Candace's pen nib nearly broke off from scribbling too fast, while even Aunt Adelaide's mouth parted in surprise.

"Death?" she said. "Whatever do you mean?"

I rubbed my forehead. "When Xavier came back to town last month, I saw him... I saw him escort someone's soul into the afterlife. I've seen the same thing again a couple of times since. Don't ask me why. Xavier was going to look into it, but so far, he hasn't found out why I can suddenly see into the afterworld."

"That, or he decided not to tell you," said Cass. "If you ask me, you never ask him anything because you're afraid he'll give you an answer you don't like."

"He wouldn't keep something like that from me," I retaliated. "What were you trying to do, drive him away from the library altogether?"

"I'm trying to help you," she snapped. "I asked him because I knew you wouldn't have the guts to do it yourself. You have to find out if this is going to work out for you long-term sooner or later, and sooner is better. Trust me."

With her book tucked under her arm, she left the room, leaving an awkward silence behind her.

"She has a point," said Aunt Candace.

"Maybe Xavier and I should get to discuss this in our own time, and not in front of someone who all but admitted she wants to use our love story in a novel?" I said. "The same someone who's playing mind games with the beta of the local werewolf pack?"

"You aren't wrong," said Aunt Adelaide. "Candace, you can't expect me to believe you didn't have a spare moment in which to tell Peter you weren't me."

"I couldn't very well bring it up in front of the patrons, could I?" she said.

"You've been with him all day!" Aunt Adelaide scowled at her sister. "You've gone too far this time. I think I'll let you dig your way out of this hole yourself. Rory, let me know if you need anything."

She swept to her feet and left the room. Aunt Candace sat down in her sister's place and began picking at her leftovers. The sound of Cass's footsteps came from upstairs. Maybe she was right, and I hadn't wanted to ruin things with Xavier by asking questions that would get me into trouble with the Grim Reaper and send our relationship back to square one again, but there was a time and a place for that and a family dinner wasn't it.

Actually, I was pretty sure there was *never* an appropriate time to ask if the Grim Reaper had ever fornicated with a human. Even on one's deathbed.

I followed Aunt Adelaide into the kitchen, where Estelle stood watching the stove. "The antidote's fine, but

I wouldn't trust Aunt Candace with it while she's in this mood."

"I'll take over," said Aunt Adelaide. "You should go to bed. You too, Rory. You've had a long day."

"Yeah." Estelle gave me a sympathetic smile as we made for the stairs. "Sorry about earlier."

"Don't be," I said. "I should have known better than to expect Aunt Candace to act normal around my boyfriend. She can't even act normal around her *own* boyfriend."

"I expected it from her," she said. "Cass, though? I'd have hoped she knew better."

"Yeah." I released a sigh. "And now the Grim Reaper has another reason to berate him for getting involved with me, if he finds out Aunt Candace is probing into the Grim Reaper's big secrets. The worst part is, she's right about me not asking the right questions."

Her mouth pressed together. "I don't blame you for taking things slow with him, considering he's immortal and you're not."

"There are some questions it's only natural to ask when you're dating someone, though," I said. "Like if they have family. I don't even know if Xavier does. I mean, I heard he came into his position through his own family, but I never thought..."

I'd never thought the Grim Reaper might be his father. I didn't see the resemblance between the two of them, but considering I'd only glimpsed the Grim Reaper's face briefly, who could say? Yet I trusted Xavier. His job made it difficult for him to confide in me, but he was doing his best to work around the Reaper's stringent rules.

"On that note," she said. "When were you going to tell us you can see into Death?"

Ah. That discussion, on the other hand, had been a long time coming. We hadn't talked in depth about how I'd seen him escorting souls into the afterlife, when humans weren't supposed to be able to see anything at all.

"I don't know," I said. "Maybe it's like when a normal sees something magical. I couldn't see magic at all before I used it by accident. Is there an equivalent for Reapers?"

"I don't know," she said. "I guess it can happen, but I swear we don't have Reaper ancestry in the family, and I don't know why else you might have ended up seeing what you did."

"I never saw it until a month ago, besides," I added. "The first time was with Mr Spencer's death at the hotel. Then Mr Blake. Then those ghosts a few weeks ago."

"But not before then?" she said. "That makes it unlikely you're part Reaper, then. I keep forgetting how many dead bodies you've stumbled across. If you weren't dating the Reaper, I'd find it worrying, to be honest."

"Ha," I said. "I only hope we *are* still dating at all, after that."

7

After a restless night, I checked the planner I kept on my bedside table and found an unwelcome reminder that I had a magic lesson with Aunt Candace this morning. After her antics at dinner yesterday, the last thing I wanted to do was spend more time in her company.

"Maybe I should pretend I have flu," I said aloud. "I doubt she'd take that excuse, right, Jet?"

The little crow flitted onto my bedside table. "Should I tell her, partner?"

I looked at the planner and sighed. "Nope. I do need to keep up with my lessons in practical magic. Maybe it won't be that bad."

I showered and dressed and went downstairs to the classroom, only to walk into Aunt Candace heading the other way.

"There is no lesson today," said Aunt Candace. "I am going to see Peter and I'm going to tell him the truth."

"Oh," I said. "Good. You do that."

Aunt Adelaide must have talked some sense into her, then. I wasn't about to complain about the cancelled lesson, either, given that Aunt Candace's teaching style tended to involve her lecturing me about whatever subject she was currently researching. Considering her current obsession with coaxing out the Reaper's secrets, she'd only end up annoying me even more if we stayed in the same room.

Xavier hadn't texted me overnight, not that that necessarily meant anything, considering the library's signal competed with the cemetery's reception as to which could be the slowest. I'd received messages up to a week late before. He wasn't annoyed with me, just my family, but that didn't make me feel any less guilty for subjecting him to their questioning. I'd have to make it up to him later.

In the meantime, I got on with practising camouflage spells, but without anyone to supervise, my attention kept slipping. After last night's fiasco, I hadn't had the mental space to dwell on yesterday's discoveries about Harris's Cupid shenanigans, but we were still no closer to finding out what was really going on.

Tyler showed up as I joined Estelle at the front desk, his costume looking surprisingly pristine after yesterday's soaking.

"Are there supposed to be no letters in the box?" he asked.

Estelle picked up the cardboard box on the desk. "Huh. Weird. I could have sworn there were a few waiting to be delivered earlier."

"Maybe everyone's already got it over with," he said.

"Perhaps they all left their letters in the box at the beginning of the week, to make sure they reached the recipient before Valentine's Day."

"I'll see if it fell out during the night." Estelle crouched to look underneath the desk. "No… nothing down here. There must be some people who left it until the last minute, surely."

"Maybe." He glanced over at the students. "I'd ask them, but I don't want to get firebombed again."

"You won't," Estelle reassured him. "Let me know if you're having trouble and I'll come and help you out."

"Sure." Cupid headed over to the students gathering at the back of the ground floor, with a resigned air as though he was walking to his own execution.

"I suppose everyone already has their dates for the party tonight," I said. "It's at the town hall, right?"

"Yes, and my mum's supposed to be meeting this vampire there for their date," Estelle said. "Assuming Aunt Candace doesn't screw it up for both of them."

Raised voices came from over by the tables near the Reading Corner. "Uh-oh."

"Cupid." Estelle dropped the box. "I'll straighten them out."

"Jet," I called to my familiar. "Can you watch the desk for a second?"

The little crow fluttered into view, landing on top of the empty box. "I will, partner!"

"Thanks." I followed Estelle towards the raised voices, where Tyler stood face to face with a huge male student who looked like a younger version of the werewolf Aunt Candace was allegedly dating.

"I didn't give her the letter!" Tyler was saying. "You must have got me confused with Harris."

"You delivered it yesterday," said the blond werewolf, his hands clenched at his sides. "Where'd you get it?"

"I don't—" Tyler shot Estelle a relieved look. "He's insisting I delivered a note to his crush from some other guy yesterday."

"The note didn't fall out of the sky and land in her lap," said the werewolf. "She was supposed to be *my* date to the party tonight. We both signed up at the blind dating service the same week."

"Calm down," Estelle said placatingly. "Whatever the issue, the delivery service is intended to be in good fun, and it isn't supposed to be an excuse not to talk to one another and sort out your problems among yourselves. If you have a problem with my Cupid, then come and talk to me about it in private. No fighting in the library."

The werewolf glared at her and stalked out of the library without further argument. The students returned to their conversations, while Tyler hovered awkwardly in the background.

Estelle clapped her hands. "Is anyone interested in sending a letter to someone they admire? Free service, guaranteed to reach the recipient before Valentine's Day."

A number of disinterested mumbles responded. Clearly, delivering Valentine's day cards was not on anyone's mind today, especially after what they'd just witnessed.

The sound of the library doors opening echoed through the lobby, and I turned around in time to see an elf and two trolls walk in. "It's Edwin. I'll go and talk to him."

"Thanks, Rory," said Estelle. "Send him my way if he needs me."

I hurried over to the chief of police, who wore a scowl on his face. "Something wrong?"

"Mrs Jones has been pestering me on an hourly basis since her son was hospitalised," said the elf. "She's been utterly unbearable."

I winced. "Sorry. She came into the library, too, but there's no way we can move any faster with the antidote. We're doing the best we can."

Or some of us were. Not Aunt Candace, though it was anyone's guess as to whether she'd kept her word and told Peter the truth. If she'd told him and he'd taken the news badly, she'd have already come back to the library by now.

"I gathered," said Edwin. "I also wanted to leave a note for your Cupid to deliver, but he seems to have disappeared."

"Oh, he's over there." I pointed to the Reading Corner. "Leave the note in the box and we'll sort it out."

Edwin removed a piece of folded-up paper from his coat pocket and put it in the box. "I do hope he delivers it before Valentine's Day."

"He will," I reassured him.

Both of his trolls shuffled forward and also dropped folded-up letters into the box. Then, without further comment, the three of them left the library.

"Well, that was unexpected," I said. "Jet, can you—"

I broke off. The crow wasn't sitting on the desk where I'd left him. Maybe he'd got distracted and flown off. I was about to go looking for him when a young woman with dark hair walked over from the direction of my family's living quarters.

"Excuse me?" I called. "Can I help you?"

"Hey," she said. "I'm Hayley. I'm here to see your aunt."

Hayley Sutton. She was the mastermind behind the blind dating service, I'd heard, though we'd never said a word to one another before. "Ah, she's not around at the moment."

"I'm from the blind dating service," she added. "There was a mix-up with the dates this week and I wanted to tell your aunts."

"Oh, they know," I said. "Both of them."

Her brow wrinkled. "I saw Candace Hawthorn with Peter Barley yesterday, and I wanted to check she's aware that she was originally slated to be paired with a different person."

"Don't worry, she's perfectly aware of it." *Unfortunately.* "They're going to clear the matter up before the party tonight."

"Oh, good." She glanced around the library, her gaze lingering on the posters adorning the balconies advertising the upcoming poetry night and the balloons floating up to the ceiling. "Where did you get those balloons?"

"We found them in a spare room in the library," I said. "Why?"

"I wondered if I'd misplaced some of ours," she said. "They're the exact same design."

"They're shaped like hearts." What else did she expect Valentine's balloons to look like? Her hostile tone was a tad unwarranted, to say the least.

"So they are." Her lips pursed. "I suppose Estelle thinks she thought of the theme first.'

"What do you mean by that?"

When Estelle herself walked into view from behind the stacks, Hayley gave me a final glare, then turned around and left the library.

"Hey, Rory." Estelle approached the desk. "Who was that?"

"Hayley Sutton, from the blind dating service," I said. "Did Aunt Adelaide say whether she was still going to the party tonight? Because Hayley found out about the mix-up."

"I don't know," said Estelle. "I mean, there's no point in her going out with her original partner, even if Aunt Candace does tell him the truth. What did she want? Just to set the record straight?"

"That, and she seemed to take offence at your balloons. She thinks you copied her design."

Her brow wrinkled. "What, is she trademarking heart-shaped balloons? Weird."

"That or Valentine's Day itself," I commented. "She seemed ticked off at your posters advertising the poetry night, too. Maybe she thinks you'll steal all her business."

"Does she think she owns the date?" Estelle shook her head. "I'm thinking of cancelling the poetry night, actually. I wouldn't have scheduled it in the first place if I'd known people would rather argue with one another than send nice love notes. At this rate, there'll be a brawl."

"Don't cancel it," I said. "Look, you have three notes to deliver right there. Edwin paid a visit."

"Really?" She picked up the box. "I'll give them to Cupid. Or maybe I should just deliver them myself."

"If you do, I wouldn't wear wings or carry arrows," I said. "Just in case."

She grimaced. "Good call."

Estelle and Cupid both left the library, while I remained on the desk. Presumably, people were busy getting ready for the party tonight, because the library remained fairly quiet. Xavier kept trying to intrude on my thoughts, and while I wouldn't see him walking around if the Grim Reaper had him under house arrest, it didn't stop me from looking up hopefully every time the door opened.

Hayley's visit hadn't helped my mood, nor had Cupid's odd dilemma. It seemed weird for people to blame one person for their own love drama—or rather, two people. Even if Harris had been behind some of the mix-ups, there was no reason to drag Tyler into it, too. But the students' accusations were a reminder that an awful lot of the people who'd been targeted by Harris had also used Hayley's blind dating services. Maybe I should have asked her about it earlier.

After half an hour, Estelle returned to the library, minus Cupid. "Tyler went home," she said. "I gave him the rest of the day off, poor guy. I think everyone's busy getting ready for the party."

"Better than dealing with the ruckus upstairs." Aunt Adelaide approached us, picking a handful of glitter out of her hair.

"What happened this time?" asked Estelle. "Cass's animals escaped again?

"Unfortunately," she said. "It seems they took objection to all the glitter and raised a fuss."

"Oh, no," I said. "You missed Hayley Sutton earlier. She came here to see you and Aunt Candace and explain what was going on with the mix-up, but Aunt Candace said she'd sort the situation out herself."

"She did?" she said. "That makes a change. Where's Cupid?"

"Gone home," said Estelle. "We've had no cards to deliver today—except from Edwin and the trolls, that is."

"Edwin was here?" she said. "I'm surprised he didn't want to check up on the antidote."

"No… well, he did tell me that Mrs Jones is now hassling the police instead of us," I said. "Also, who's watching the antidote at the moment?"

"Sylvester," said Aunt Adelaide. "I assumed Candace was slacking off on duty, but this apology is taking a long time."

"Did you expect her to go through with it?" Estelle rolled her eyes. "I'll take these returns upstairs."

"And I'll get back to the antidote." Aunt Adelaide crossed the library to our living quarters, while I remained behind the desk.

A moment later, the sound of loud cursing echoed from the direction of the kitchen.

"Aunt Candace?" I hurried across the library and into our family living quarters—then stared through the kitchen door.

The cauldron lay face-down, the remains of the antidote strewn across the floor. Aunt Adelaide stood over it, swearing loudly. There was no sign of Sylvester.

"How?" I breathed. "Who did that?"

"Whoever it was, they did it on purpose," said Aunt Adelaide. "They didn't want Harris waking up."

"His mother is going to kill us." I glanced behind me,

looking for Estelle. "Edwin said she's been hassling him ever since Estelle stopped her from pestering us."

"This is my fault," said Aunt Adelaide. "I should have known Candace would get bored, and I should have known better than to put the owl in charge while she was gone."

"What's your fault?" Estelle entered the room and clapped her hands to her mouth. "Oh, no."

"Can you save it?" I crouched beside the spilled potion, but its colour had already turned dull grey rather than its previous bright colour. "Any of it?"

"No," said Aunt Adelaide. "I'm afraid the only option is to start from scratch."

"Who came in here?" Estelle crossed the room, her expression distraught.

"I'd blame Sylvester, but even he isn't *that* mean." I glanced up at the cupboards where he sometimes perched. "Where'd he go, anyway?"

"I told him to fly directly down from the third floor to watch the potion while I helped Cass with her animals," said Aunt Adelaide. "He must have got distracted on the way. I'll clear this up. You two—look around, see if you can find who might have done this."

Estelle backed out of the room, pressing the heels of her hands into her eyes. "Anyone who came into the library after Aunt Candace went out might have been responsible. We should never have mentioned we were working on it at all."

"We should talk to them," I said. "Jet, where are you?"

"Here, partner!" he squeaked, flying up to the kitchen door. "Oh no, oh no!"

"Did you see who did this?"

"No, partner." He flew in agitated circles above my head.

"Can you go and find Sylvester?" I asked. "He was supposed to be watching the antidote."

"Of course." He zoomed off into the library, while Estelle and I followed more slowly.

"We should put a watch on our living quarters from now on," Estelle said. "People come in and out all the time —but I didn't expect anyone to break into our kitchen to sabotage us on purpose."

Some of the students had noticed the ruckus and were on their feet, wandering around the lobby. Roy James spotted me and made his way over. "What's the fuss about?"

I halted in front of him and his mates. "Have any of you been into the kitchen? In our living quarters?"

"Why?" asked Roy.

"Someone spilled the antidote," I explained. "The antidote we were brewing to wake up Harris. Did you see anyone hanging around near the stairs?"

"No," he said. "Most people already went home, to get ready for the party at the town hall tonight."

"All right. Thanks."

The cawing of an owl sounded, and Sylvester swooped down from the balcony.

"Sylvester." Estelle hurried to accost him. "Where have you been? Someone spilled the antidote."

"He was sleeping on the stairs," Jet squeaked.

"Tell-tale," said the owl.

"Someone broke into our family's living quarters and knocked over the cauldron while you were meant to be watching it." Estelle's face reddened. "What do you mean, you were sleeping?"

Jet flew to my shoulder, where I gave him a stroke. "Can you keep an eye on the entrance to our living quarters from now on? If anyone who isn't part of our family tries to enter, you have permission to peck them."

"Of course, partner!" he said.

Not that it was any use now. Sylvester flew back to the kitchen, followed by Estelle and me. Roy was right—most of the students had already left the library. It seemed half the town would be attending tonight's party, and none of them knew who'd knocked over the antidote.

We re-entered the kitchen, where Aunt Adelaide had cleared up the spilt potion with a wave of her wand and set the cauldron back on the stove.

"Did the person who did this leave any traces behind?" I asked.

"Not that I can find," said Aunt Adelaide, moving piles of ingredients around the table. "Did any of the students strike you as suspicious?"

"No," I said, "but there aren't many people around, and everyone's distracted by tonight's party."

"Did you say Hayley visited earlier?" asked Aunt Adelaide.

"She did," I said. "She also seemed to think she owned the Valentine's theme and Estelle was copying her, which is bizarre."

"It's not like I've kept it a secret," said Estelle. "Why, you don't think *she* might have sabotaged us, do you?"

"She was hanging around here earlier for a while before I noticed her," I remembered. "I should have paid more attention."

The person responsible must have already been in the

library, because I'd have seen them come through the door if they hadn't been. If not the students or the other patrons, then Hayley certainly fit the criteria. But her attitude earlier didn't necessarily make her guilty.

"Really." Her brow wrinkled. "I've never met her before. I also hadn't heard of her being involved in social events until she started putting up posters advertising her blind dating service. Are you still going to the party, Mum?"

"If I am, Candace isn't," Aunt Adelaide said. "Unless one of you wants to volunteer to watch the antidote. I won't take any more chances."

"I'll watch it," said Estelle. "It should have been my responsibility from the start, considering Cupid was shot on my watch. I should talk to his mother, too."

"You don't need to take the burden all on yourself," I protested. "Get Cass to watch the antidote. I doubt she'll be going to the party."

Estelle cleared her throat. Ah. Cass was standing right behind me, with Sylvester perched on her shoulder. He did not look contrite in the slightest.

"Maybe I have other plans," said Cass. "Which don't involve dressing up in ridiculous costumes. Besides, who wants to hang out with my mother and aunt and their romantic partners all night?"

"I'm in two minds about whether to go," said Aunt Adelaide. "I would prefer not to be in the vicinity of Candace if it turns out she *hasn't* told Peter the truth."

Cass rolled her eyes. "Is it true that someone knocked over the antidote?"

"Yeah, but it might have been anyone," I said. "Sylvester was supposed to be watching it."

I gave the owl a pointed look, but he closed his eyes. "I naturally sleep during the day, you know. It's cruel to expect me to stay awake."

"You sleep whenever it suits you," Aunt Adelaide corrected. "I'll restart the antidote myself. Are there any students still in the library?"

"Not many," I said. "But it might have happened at any point after you left the kitchen."

"After I…" she broke off. "Someone left open the door to Cass's animals' room and let them out. I wonder if they did it to distract us."

I turned to Cass. "Do you think they did?"

"If they did, they'll be spending the night in the manticore's cage," she said.

"I thought you didn't have the manticore any longer," I said. "It seems a stretch that someone sneaked up to the third floor to divert your attention so they could wreck the antidote. They'd have had to be confident Estelle and I wouldn't go into the kitchen either."

"And that Sylvester would slack off," added Estelle. "It sounds more like someone took advantage of the first opportunity to get close to the antidote and got lucky."

"Slacking off!" said the owl. "What have you been doing to keep the place running? I am in charge of all the late fees, and a lot more besides. And just where is Candace at the moment?"

"Telling her date tonight her real identity." I narrowed my eyes. "Which wouldn't have been necessary if you'd let *me* tell him instead of interrupting."

"Candace is dealing with it herself, so there's no harm done," said the owl.

"Except for our antidote," I reminded him. "Someone

got into our family living quarters because nobody was paying attention—someone who knew we were brewing an antidote."

"And what do you expect me to do about that?" he said.

I was tempted to ask the Forbidden Room, which held answers about all the books in the library, but not about the people who came *into* the library. Nor how their romantic entanglements might have led to someone shooting Cupid and spilling the antidote.

"I expect you to give me a hand with this," Aunt Adelaide said. "No funny business this time."

The owl hooted. "I don't see you flinging the blame at Candace."

"She'll get an earful when she's back," said Aunt Adelaide. "Estelle, Rory, can one of you watch the desk? I'll get on with sorting out the ingredients."

"Starting from scratch," Estelle muttered to herself. "I can't believe this. Was Hayley really hanging around near the stairs?"

I thought back. "She was. I don't know her, and I don't want to jump to conclusions, but considering her comments about the balloons…"

And then there was the fact that most of the people who'd fallen victim to Harris's pranks had used her blind dating service. Granted, it was the only blind dating service in town, but still.

On a whim, I texted Xavier asking him to go with me to the party tonight to find out if I was worried over nothing. This time, the reply came almost instantly: *Sorry, my boss has me doing paperwork all night. See you tomorrow?*

Sure.

Great. If I went to see him in person, the Grim Reaper would probably answer the door and tell me to go away. Even I had too much pride left to beg the Angel of Death to let his apprentice come to a party with me.

But that didn't mean I couldn't go alone.

8

"Invisibility?" said Estelle. "Are you sure?"

"It's not invisibility," I said. "It's camouflage. I haven't been able to get the hang of the spell yet, so this is an extra incentive for me to practise."

I'd rather have gone out with Xavier, but I didn't want Aunt Adelaide to spend her date looking over her shoulder for signs of trouble. Hayley's weird behaviour earlier had drawn out my suspicions, and the least I could do was ensure she wouldn't do anything to cause trouble for my family.

"Maybe, but going alone to a party isn't much fun," she said.

"I'm not going for the same reasons as everyone else," I said. "I just want to make sure nothing dodgy is going on. Hayley's one of the few people in town who *does* have access to the details of people's love lives."

Or some of them, anyway. Besides, half the students who'd been in the library would also be attending the party, so maybe I'd witness something which would enable me to put the pieces together more easily. As little as I felt like leaving the library, I was too restless even to sit quietly and read after what had happened to the antidote.

"All right," said Estelle. "I'll watch your wand-work and tell you if you're doing it right, okay?"

I raised my wand and moved it in the complex motion I'd been practising. A light flashed, and a gust of wind raised the hair from my forehead. When I looked down, my body was no longer there.

"Perfect," said Estelle. "If anyone uses a revealing spell on you, it'll undo the effect, but they'll probably only do that if they realise there's someone there."

"I'll try my best not to knock into anyone, then," I said. "And I'll stay away from the dance floor."

Aunt Adelaide sailed into the room, wearing a flowery dress worthy of Aunt Candace, with her hair curled impeccably and her face carefully made up. She gave a startled jump when I waved my wand and undid the camouflage spell. "Goddess, Rory. I didn't know you could use that spell yet. I know Candace has been neglecting your lessons."

"I've been practising." I lowered my wand. "Ready for your date, then?"

"I am," she said. "I assume Candace won't be around. Has she been with Peter all day?"

"Seems so," said Estelle. "Not sure if she told him her real identity or not, but she sure seems attached to him considering she was expecting to go on a date with someone else."

"If I didn't know better, I'd say she's infatuated," said Aunt Adelaide. "She doesn't typically go for werewolves at all, let alone those who are high in the pack hierarchy. Says it's not worth the hassle."

"That's why I'm surprised they paired you up to begin with," said Estelle. "Rory is going to the party, too, by the way. But she'll be invisible."

"I'm going to do some snooping," I explained. "It might be a coincidence, but I'm seeing a lot of overlap between the people who had a problem with Harris and the people who used Hayley's services."

"Hmm," said Aunt Adelaide. "I'll keep an eye out, too. It worries me that she picked a fight with you earlier, Rory."

"You don't have to spend your date watching out for trouble," I said. "There might not be any. It's a hunch, that's all. As for Aunt Candace, I'll try to keep an eye on her, too, if she shows her face. She might well be avoiding us because she thinks we'll blame her for the antidote."

"She wouldn't be wrong." Aunt Adelaide tutted. "All right. Follow close behind me, Rory. Camouflaged or not, I wouldn't walk around alone after dark."

"The biggest danger is me tripping over my own feet." I was already having second thoughts, but if I changed my mind by the time I got to the town hall, I could just sneak back to the library without anyone noticing. No need to make excuses to get out of a party when nobody could see you.

Aunt Candace hadn't returned to the library yet, so I didn't know how her conversation with Peter had gone. Maybe we'd luck out and she and Aunt Adelaide wouldn't cross paths tonight after all. Had she even heard about the antidote? If she had, then perhaps she wanted to avoid the fallout. Then again, it was just like Aunt Candace to have been distracted with her new sweetheart and completely fail to notice anything was going on.

We made our way through the square to the town hall, which was covered in full Valentine's décor on both the inside and the outside. I counted at least a dozen Cupids wandering around, most of whom wore wings and carried bows and arrows. It seemed recent events hadn't deterred them in the slightest, but perhaps they assumed they'd be safe at the party.

I scanned the crowd for Aunt Candace and spotted her and the werewolf having a rather non-verbal conversation in the corner. I averted my gaze, my heart sinking. Had she still not told him the truth? It was impossible to tell, but he didn't seem to mind either way.

Given the stony expression on Aunt Adelaide's face, the same thought had crossed her mind. I definitely wasn't going to walk into the middle of that one, so I settled for scanning the room in search of anyone else who looked familiar.

"Excuse me," said a polite, cultured voice, addressing Aunt Adelaide. A tall man stepped over to her, faster than any normal human could move. If his speed didn't give the game away, his elegant style of dress and waxwork-like complexion painted him as a vampire.

After a spate of recent brushes with death involving the vampires, let's just say I was a little edgy around them. Even the vampires in town who supposedly obeyed the rules rallied around Evangeline, who was currently miffed at me for 'choosing' to side with the Grim Reaper over her. Thankfully, the leader of the vampires didn't appear to be at the party.

The vampire might have been able to sniff me out with

his super-senses even while I was under the camouflage spell, but thankfully, his gaze was fixed on Aunt Adelaide with an expression of great interest. "Are you Candace Hawthorn?"

"No, I'm Adelaide," she said. "There was a misunderstanding, and my sister and I switched dates. She's with the werewolf over there. I hope you don't mind."

"Not at all." The vampire smiled, showing a flash of fangs. "Shall we?"

He took her arm and they walked away together, leaving me feeling slightly deflated at the reminder of Xavier's habit of placing one hand on my arm as we walked together. I didn't believe we were finished, far from it, but I was starting to wish I'd opted to stay in and read a book instead of being the sole single person at a party aimed at lovestruck couples.

My gaze landed on Hayley, who sat at a table near the door, talking to a tall guy dressed as Cupid. As I started to head that way, someone jostled my elbow, sending me tripping over my feet. I caught my balance on a table, causing the drinks to clank against one another, but luckily, none of them spilt on the floor.

I moved forward, more careful this time, and found my suspicion confirmed: the person talking to Hayley was Taylor, our current Cupid.

"That Hawthorn witch put you up to this, didn't she?" she was saying, in an accusing voice.

"No, I came here on my own account," he said. "I didn't know I was banned from the town hall."

"Don't give me that tone," she said. "I fired you for a reason. Did you think I'd welcome you back here with open arms now you've been scheming with that Hawthorn witch against me?"

Uh-oh. I hovered awkwardly in the background, shooting a glance at Aunt Candace. She looked like she had no intention of moving… which at least ought to mean she'd leave Aunt Adelaide and her date alone.

But Hayley's words alarmed me. She seemed to think she and Estelle had a history, which was news to me. I'd also thought Tyler had quit, not been fired.

The door blew open with a gust of air, and a sudden spate of screams drifted in.

"Murder!" someone shouted from outside.

My heart lurched as the crowd surged towards the doors, propelling me along with them. Several people bumped into me, but they were too intent on getting outside to notice they'd collided with an invisible person.

Outside the doors, Morris Wilson lay still on the ground, an arrow sticking out of his shoulder.

"He's dead!" screamed the girl at his side. "He just fell. Someone shot him."

I hadn't thought he'd dare show up here after the very public scene with his ex-girlfriend and the girl he'd been crushing on, though neither of them seemed to be around. Not that it was easy to tell, with the crowd erupting from the pub, trailing glitter and heart-shaped balloons everywhere.

"He's not dead," someone said. "It's like Harris all over again—he's been knocked out cold."

More shouting came from further down the road. My stomach sank at the sight of a second body lying a few feet away—Carey Landon, who lay on her back with an arrow sticking out of her own shoulder.

"Someone's picking us off!" said a hysterical voice.

"Calm down!" Hayley said. "I'll call the hospital. And the police."

What with the panicking crowd running amok through the street, it was impossible to get close enough to Carey's body to look at the arrow, but it appeared to be identical to the one Morris had been shot with. The person responsible must be somewhere outside, but the chaos made it impossible to tell who'd already been out in the street and who'd come out of the town hall when they'd heard the shouting. It didn't help that half of them were in costume, while more than a few were carrying fake arrows, too.

I'd lost sight of my aunts, but camouflaged or not, I wasn't doing myself any favours by sticking around here. Sooner or later, someone would realise there was an invisible person trying to sneak into the crime scene.

I extricated myself from the crowd and hurried back towards the library—then I halted at the sight of a blond figure approaching me. My heart gave a flip. "Xavier?"

"Rory." He looked at me, confusion etched on his features. "Where are you? I can hear you, but I can't see you."

Oh. Right. I quickly pulled out my wand and undid the camouflage spell. "I'm undercover. I thought *you* were under house arrest."

"My boss sent me to see what was going on." He jerked his head towards the town hall. "He heard the noise from the cemetery. You were at the party?"

"I was kind of spying on them," I admitted. "But then someone shot two of the guests with arrows, just like Harris. I wanted to get a closer look, but there are too many people panicking and running around. The person who did it might be in the crowd, or they might have gone, for all I know."

"Then you shouldn't stick around." He took my arm. "I'll walk you home."

"The library's right over there," I protested automatically, though after the disastrous dinner with my family, just seeing him again made me feel miles better.

Xavier and I reached the doorstep to the library, and he embraced me briefly. "I wouldn't come outside again until the coast is clear, Rory."

"I wasn't planning to," I said. "Oh, and I'm sorry about last night."

"Don't be," he said. "You should get some sleep. Text me if you need me, okay?"

"I will." I wanted to say more, but the crowd had begun to swarm across the square, and I wasn't invisible any longer. "See you later."

He turned and walked away into the night, disappearing with the swift feet of a Reaper.

9

The following morning, I woke with glitter all over myself and no clue how it'd got there. I hadn't even touched anyone at the party, or so I thought. Maybe it'd landed on me when I'd been jostled by the crowd leaving the pub. I reached for my wand and used a vanishing spell to make it disappear. At least my magic was working, even if my investigative abilities weren't. I'd been turning over the details of last night's event for hours and drawing a total blank.

I went down to the kitchen in search of coffee and found the antidote bubbling on the stove under Aunt Adelaide's watchful eye.

"I'm staying in here all day," she said. "Let's see anyone else try to get their hands on this antidote."

"Have you been in here all night?" I went to the table, where she'd conjured up coffee and breakfast. "You could have asked one of us to take over."

She waved a hand. "Candace was impossible, Cass

would have refused, and Estelle needed the rest. So did you, Rory."

"It wasn't like I had a late night," I protested. "What time did you get back, anyway?"

I'd assumed she and Candace had got back to the library after I'd already gone to bed, but only now did I remember that Aunt Candace might not have heard about the spilled antidote until her return.

"Not long after you did, I expect," she said. "Needless to say, I wasn't allowed near the crime scene. Nor was anyone else, once the police showed up. Alex walked me home, and that was the end of it."

"You mean the vampire?" I said. "Are you seeing him again?"

Before she could answer, Aunt Candace sauntered into the kitchen. "Hello, my dears."

Aunt Adelaide and I exchanged raised eyebrows. When Aunt Candace grabbed a piece of toast and made to leave, Aunt Adelaide snagged her arm. "Not so fast. You still haven't apologised for not being around to see who spilt the first dose on the floor."

"I could say the same of you, too," she said. "And you were *in* the library when it happened."

So Aunt Adelaide must have told her about the antidote last night. I found myself immensely glad I'd missed out on that conversation.

"You were the one who volunteered to brew it," I pointed out. "That ought to mean you should also be the one who deals with Mrs Jones. I think poor Edwin is taking the heat at the moment for the antidote not being ready, and it'll get worse if she finds out the cure is delayed a few days."

Aunt Adelaide muttered a curse under her breath. "Of course it will. I haven't seen the woman, but it wouldn't surprise me if word makes it to her ears all the same."

"Especially if she hears about yesterday's victims," I added. "Is there going to be enough of the antidote for three people?"

"Good question." Aunt Adelaide peered into the cauldron. "There should be enough to go around … provided nobody *spills* any this time."

Aunt Candace shoved half a piece of toast into her mouth in answer.

"Speaking of which," I said. "The Poison Apple itself must still be out there, if the person who shot last night's victims had more of it ready. Either that or they're brewing it up as-needed."

"Too impractical," said Aunt Adelaide at once. "No, they have a single stash of Poison Apple, no doubt hidden in their own home."

"In their home." I thought of Nova Lyle at the lab. "We can knock Carey and Morris off the suspect list now. There's still a lot of people who assume Harris screwed them over, but why would they shoot those two as well? I mean, Morris made his ex angry, but that's no reason to target Carey, too."

"We can't know for sure until they wake up," said Aunt Adelaide, giving the potion another vigorous stir. "Which I intend to ensure."

"Good luck with that." Aunt Candace marched out of the kitchen. "I am going to work on my novel. Or maybe I'll write a letter for Cupid to deliver."

"It's Valentine's Day on Monday. You'd better make it quick," I said to her retreating back.

Aunt Adelaide shook her head. "Really. She's like a lovesick schoolgirl."

"She really does like him," I murmured. "Did you get a clear answer from her about whether she told him her real name?"

"She dodged all my questions and then claimed to be distracted by how distraught she was over the antidote," said Aunt Adelaide. "I assume he does know by now. It would have come up at the party, I imagine."

"I should hope so." Estelle walked into the room, yawning. "How was your date, anyway, Mum?"

"Better than I expected," Aunt Adelaide said. "Alex certainly has the typical vampire charm, but he was a total gentleman."

"Are you seeing him again?" asked Estelle.

"Maybe," her mother replied. "Perhaps I'll make use of that Cupid of yours."

"Speaking of whom, he should be here any minute now." Estelle grabbed a piece of toast and walked out eating it. "If he wasn't at the party, that is. I think half the town will be sleeping in, based on the noise I heard from outside last night. Unless that was just Aunt Candace."

I walked after Estelle into the lobby, which looked oddly bare. Then it hit me—the posters from the balconies had gone, as had the ribbons and balloons. "What did you do with the decorations?"

"They didn't feel appropriate," she said. "Also, I'm thinking of cancelling Monday's themed poetry night. At this rate, it'll be a bloodbath."

My shoulders slumped. "But it feels like we're giving in to the person who wanted to stop Cupid."

"Maybe, but yesterday's victims were shot with arrows, too," said Estelle. "Who were the victims again?"

"Carey Landon and Morris Wilson," I said. "I don't know if anyone saw who shot them because the guests from the party swarmed out of the town hall the moment the screaming started, and I had to run home before I got caught in the crush."

"There must have been witnesses," said Estelle. "That sounds like a nightmare, though, Rory. I don't blame you for running home."

"It was dark outside and half the guests at the party were wearing Cupid costumes, which didn't help," I said. "Including Tyler."

"That'd explain why he's late." She looked up hopefully when the door opened.

It wasn't Cupid. Hayley Sutton entered, and she wore a livid expression on her face which grew even more furious when she set eyes on Estelle. "Thought you'd sabotage my party, did you?"

"I have no idea what you're talking about," she said. "I heard two of your guests were shot, though. I'm sorry."

"As though you didn't put your Cupid up to it," Hayley spat.

"He wasn't—" I broke off. If I said Taylor couldn't have possibly been the one who'd shot the victims because I'd seen them talking, I'd have to confess to using a camouflage spell to sneak into the party myself. "If Cupid did anything, it had nothing to do with us."

"Is there a problem?" Aunt Adelaide's voice drifted out of the corridor leading to our living quarters, where Jet guarded the door. She wouldn't leave the antidote unattended, not after last time.

"A likely story." Without another word, Hayley turned and left the library, leaving an awkward silence behind.

"Sorry," I said to Estelle. "I should have told you I overheard her talking to Tyler at the party. About us. It wasn't complimentary."

"She was gossiping about us behind our backs?" she said. "Why him? Did she want to convince him to work for her instead?"

"He used to work for the blind dating service, and she wasn't happy to see him in the slightest," I explained. "Sounds like he got fired, so she was convinced he purposefully signed up to work at the library to get back at her or something."

Estelle's brows rose. "What does she think I did? I swear we've never spoken before all this."

"No idea, but Tyler took a major risk showing up to the party, by the looks of things," I said. "Unless he hoped she wouldn't see him. Or he had a date himself."

"I wonder why he got fired." Estelle peered into the box on the desk. "He won't have anything to do today, unless Aunt Candace wants to send more love notes to Peter."

"At least he'd know her name then." I rolled my eyes. "I'm sure Tyler said he quit working for Hayley when there was a mix-up with people's dates and they blamed him for it. He never said he was fired."

So who was telling the truth?

The door opened again. This time, it was Cupid, carrying his fake bow and arrows over his shoulder.

"Hey," he said. "Sorry I'm late. I'm guessing you heard about the party last night?"

"You were there?" I said, deciding to feign ignorance. After all, nobody had seen me, including Tyler.

"Yeah, I went in costume," he said. "I regret it now, believe me. I had to make a run for it when those two students got shot."

Hmm. "I thought you and Hayley had bad feelings between you? She was just here in the library, and that's the impression I got, anyway. She said she fired you," I added, deciding to call his bluff.

"She would say that," he said. "I quit after one of her clients yelled at me for sending them on a date with the wrong person. What was she doing here?"

"She blames us for the incident last night," said Estelle. "Which makes no sense to me. Did the police find no leads on who shot the two students?"

"It was too dark and crowded for them to track anyone down," he said. "Drunken Cupids wandering all over town… you can imagine. Anyway, I'm going to have to lie low for a while."

"You'll be fine," I said. "If lots of people were dressed as Cupid, there's no reason for anyone to blame you."

The door opened and Edwin walked into the library. *Ah. Maybe not.*

"Hey," I said. "Ah—if you're here to check up on the antidote, I have some bad news."

"The cauldron was knocked off the stove," explained Estelle. "As soon as we realised, we started over, but we need a few extra days."

"Wait, the antidote's gone?" said Tyler. "Was it an accident?"

"No," I said. "Someone sneaked into our living quarters while we were all working and knocked the cauldron off the stove."

Edwin's laid two identical arrows on the desk. "I would appreciate if you or your aunts could help me assess these. Your aunts probably told you that two people were shot at the party at the town hall last night, and the evidence seems to point to the potion being the same as the one used against young Harris."

Cupid shuffled away from the arrows as I picked them up, as though he was afraid they'd knock him out if he got too close. "I'll take them to my aunt. Do you have any ideas about who the perpetrator might be?"

"I'm afraid not," the elf said. "We questioned everyone at the scene, but given the choice of weapon, it was impossible to pinpoint the culprit." He glanced at Cupid, who blanched.

"Of course," Estelle said sympathetically. "Let us know if you need anything else."

"I will," said Edwin. "By the way—did your Cupid deliver my letter? I haven't heard from Karen yet."

"I—yes, he did," Estelle said. "Thanks for your time."

After Edwin left, Tyler sheepishly said, "I swear I did deliver his letter."

"I'm sure you did," said Estelle. "Rory, can you take those arrows to my mum?"

"Of course." I made my way to the kitchen with the arrows, where Aunt Adelaide stood over the stove with an expression on her face which suggested that anyone who interrupted her would find themselves force-fed a dose of Poison Apple.

"Hey," I said. "Edwin wanted you to look at these arrows and confirm the potion is the same as the one used on Harris. Given the effects on the two victims, it must be."

"He didn't have anything to say about the possible culprits?" she said.

"No." I dropped the arrows on the table. "Too many people wearing Cupid costumes, apparently. Did everyone buy their arrows from the same costume shop?"

Her forehead scrunched up. "There *is* only one costume shop in town, *Dress to Enchant.*"

No wonder the Cupids' costumes and arrows all looked the same.

"Anyway, if they were trying to get Hayley to blame us, it worked," I added. "Tyler didn't help by going to the party dressed in costume, too, but I don't know why Hayley's blaming Estelle. Did you talk to her last night at all?"

"No," she said. "You and Estelle will keep an eye out for trouble while I'm in here, won't you?"

"Of course," I said. "And Jet will watch the corridor outside."

I left the arrows in the kitchen and went to check on Jet, who landed on my shoulder and nibbled my ear affectionately. I gave him a stroke and returned to the lobby, finding Tyler had left. Cupid had been spared another day, but Carey and Morris were officially off the suspect list. That left a great deal of other romantically scorned individuals, but the targets of last night's attacks seemed plain weird. Harris being shot at least made sense, but neither of the others was responsible for delivering Valentine's cards. The odds of the perpetrator being someone different weren't high either, given how difficult and expensive the potion was to brew.

My thoughts went back to Nova and the alchemy lab, but I'd found no signs of Poison Apple inside the lab when I'd looked around. Still, I'd need to talk to the students again if I wanted to gather any more clues.

I re-joined Estelle at the desk, where she gave me a weak smile. "I suppose I should be grateful the law is on my side. Edwin believes me."

"Hayley didn't complain to him about us, did she?" I asked.

"She mentioned my name last night when the police showed up at the venue," she murmured. "It's a good job they didn't pass one another on their way here."

"True." No students had shown up yet, nor anyone else either. "Everyone must be sleeping in, recovering from last night. Or under the effects of Poison Apple."

"Carey Landon was one of the victims, right?" she said. "Zee *just* got a new apprentice. I bet she's not happy."

"I doubt she is," I said. "Where'd Cupid go?"

"I told him to come back in an hour," she said. "With nobody here, there's no point in him hanging around in costume all day. Especially with Hayley on the warpath."

"No kidding," I said. "I wish Edwin had been able to gather more clues from the scene. The person responsible must have been counting on half the crowd being in costume to mask them from view."

"Yeah." She flipped open the logbook, looking preoccupied. "He said there were a fair few fights that broke out after they closed the town hall. I wish I could do something to resolve all these bad feelings."

"I think that's out of our control until the victims wake up," I said. "But if you've got any ideas, I'd be happy to help you out."

"If I think of anything, I'll let you know. Best to wait until the victims wake up. Carey… and Morris. Did they know one another?"

"They were both on the suspect list, but that's all they had in common." I'd thought it over a dozen times since last night, but I'd drawn no new conclusions. "Morris caused a fair bit of drama, but I didn't see his ex at the party. She didn't know Carey, either, I don't think."

Estelle shook her head. "I'm surprised Morris was even there. Carey, too. Why would they go to a Valentine's party for couples if they just broke up with their respective significant others?"

"Free drinks," I suggested. "And the chance of a hookup? I don't know, I'm just throwing out suggestions. The targets seem totally random, too."

Why pick those particular victims? They had nothing in common but their link to Harris, and that was a tenuous one. It might seem like half the people Harris had an issue with were at the party, but in a small town like this one without much in the way of nightlife, nearly everyone who wanted to go out on a Friday night would have been there.

Estelle's mouth pressed together. "Maybe it *was* random. Perhaps the person who shot Harris gave someone else the same idea. That, or Mrs Jones went on a rampage because she was mad about the antidote taking longer than planned."

"Can you imagine her going to a party?" I said. "In a Cupid's outfit with wings?"

Estelle snorted loudly, then both of us jumped when the door opened. For a heartbeat, I worried it was the woman herself, summoned up by our words, but instead, a tall blond stranger stalked into the library.

"Hey," said Estelle brightly. "Can I help you?"

The woman stormed up to Estelle. "What do you mean by delivering me a note from Edwin addressed to Karen Thompson?"

"Who?" Estelle blinked at her.

"We broke up last week," said the woman. "But I guess his apology isn't worth much if he can't even get my name right."

She threw a piece of paper on the desk, and without further ado, she turned and marched out of the library.

"What was that about?" I asked.

"No idea," Estelle said. "The name Karen Thompson rings a bell, but I thought the note Edwin left had a different name on it. I'll have to check with Tyler."

"Well, *you* can't have made a mistake, considering Edwin is the one who wrote the note," I said. "He broke up with that woman, then?"

"Apparently." Estelle looked down at the paper. "I could have sworn this was addressed to someone else when I first saw it."

"You don't think someone switched out the names again?" I read the note over her shoulder. It did look like the elf's handwriting. "It doesn't sound like Edwin, sending a lovelorn note to another woman right after a brutal breakup."

Her brow furrowed. "I'll have to wait until Tyler comes back to ask him. I'm starting to think I was right in cancelling the poetry night, considering everything Valentine's-themed seems to be cursed with bad luck."

"No kidding." We didn't seem to be having much luck

in the visitor department today either. "At least most of the confetti has gone."

"I used a cleaning spell." She exhaled in a sigh. "Oh, and nobody put the returns away yet."

"I'll do it." I turned to the box beside the desk and picked up the topmost book. "This is from the ground floor. Won't take a minute."

I carried the book through to the Reading Corner, reading the number on the spine telling me where to shelve it. Finding the right shelf, I climbed the ladder and pushed the book into place.

"Boo," said Sylvester.

I jumped off the ladder, falling on my rear. Luckily, I landed on a beanbag and not on the floor. "What was that in aid of?"

The owl hooted with laughter. "Your face, Aurora."

"You're a menace." I rubbed my knee, which had hit something hard when I'd landed. The beanbag rattled when I rose to my feet. Frowning, I moved it aside and exposed a smaller carrier bag lying underneath.

I lifted the bag, and Sylvester released a squawk of alarm when an arrow fell out and tumbled to the carpet. Another dozen identical arrows filled the bag, too.

Cupid's arrows. Who had hidden them back here?

10

I lifted the bag of arrows carefully, in case they were covered in Poison Apple, too. They were definitely the same design as the ones Cupid had used, but they weren't the ones he'd been carrying when I'd seen him earlier. So who'd left them in the Reading Corner?

I picked up the one which had fallen to the floor. "Don't just stand there and gawk, Sylvester. Help me."

"What do you expect me to do?" He flapped his wings. "Also, I'm not standing."

"Now is not the time to be pedantic." I shooed him away. "Go on, make yourself useful and see if there are any more runaway arrows hidden around the library."

In the meantime, I carried the bag through into the kitchen. "Aunt Adelaide, I found these hidden under a beanbag in the Reading Corner."

She gave them a brief glance and turned back to the stove. "Did your Cupid leave them there?"

"Maybe, but which one?" My gaze snagged on the two

arrows lying on the table, the ones Edwin had given me earlier. "Did you check those?"

The potion on the stove hissed and spat. I stepped back out of range, catching a whiff of yarrow roots.

Aunt Adelaide muttered a curse and waved her wand over the cauldron. "I'm not as much of a natural at this as Candace is—*why* can't she see this is more important than her little dalliances?"

"Hey, Mum." Estelle walked into the kitchen, her eyes going straight to the bag of arrows in my hand. "Where'd those come from?"

"I found them hidden in the Reading Corner," I said. "Did you see Tyler head over there earlier?"

"No." Her brow furrowed. "Perhaps someone left their props behind before going to the party yesterday."

"That's what I thought, but it's weird timing." Though as Estelle had rightly pointed out earlier, there *was* only one costume shop in town, so all the arrows looked the same for a reason. "I found them underneath a beanbag, and I wouldn't have known they were there if Sylvester hadn't thought it was funny to frighten me into falling off a ladder."

"That owl," said Aunt Adelaide. "I'll look at the arrows, Rory. And I'll have a word with Sylvester, the next time I see him."

"I sent him to fly around looking for more arrows." I laid the bag down on the table. "Just in case."

Estelle picked up an arrow and dropped it again. "You don't think they're covered in Poison Apple, too?"

"Unless I'm mistaken, someone didn't want them to be found."

"Wait." Estelle's eyes went wide. "What if someone

wanted to set us up? Hayley Sutton already thinks we're responsible for wrecking her party."

"Hayley is irrational and jealous," I said. "There's zero proof. And I *saw* Tyler at the party at the same moment those two students were shot with arrows, so she can't pin the blame on either of the people we've hired. He couldn't have done it."

Estelle sat down at the kitchen table. "I think I'd remember doing anything to tick her off."

"It's not you," I said. "Believe me, the problem is all on her end."

She slumped in her seat. "We're the ones losing business."

"Tell you what, I'll go and fetch us a snack from Zee's place." I left the arrows and climbed to my feet. "I can talk to her about Carey while I'm at it and ask who might have had a reason to target her."

"Sure," said Estelle. "Go ahead. I'll handle the arrows."

"Who's going to watch the front desk?" Aunt Adelaide asked.

"I'll see if Cass is around." I walked back into the lobby. "Jet, where are you?"

"Here, partner!" he said, flying over.

"Can you fetch Cass to watch the desk?" I asked. "Tell her to come downstairs."

"Of course!" He took flight for the third floor, while I headed out of the library. Few people were in the square, but my mood improved at the smell of Zee's baking, even if Zee herself looked a little worse for wear.

"Hey." I closed the bakery door behind me. "I heard about Carey. Sorry."

"I'm starting to think I'm cursed to keep losing my

apprentices." She scurried to fetch my usual order, putting muffins into a bag. "At least she'll wake up in a day or two."

"Ah… it'll be a little longer than that," I said. "My aunt's brewing the antidote, but someone knocked the cauldron off the stove yesterday, so we had to start from scratch."

"Seriously?" she said. "Why would they do that?"

"It's kind of what I wanted to ask you," I admitted. "I mean, I came here to buy a snack, too. But Carey… she used to date Harris, the first person who was targeted."

"Oh yeah, I remember you came to talk to her," she said. "Did you guess she might be next?"

"I didn't, no," I said. "She was on the suspect list initially because she knew Harris, but it looks like everyone else did, too. I wondered if you'd seen or heard anything when she was working here which might hint at why someone would choose to target her."

"Nothing." She put the bag on the counter, and I handed over the cash for the muffins. "She was a great employee. Always on time. I didn't ask her about Harris. Figured it wasn't any of my business."

I thought back to who else they'd both been acquainted with. Roy James, maybe. I couldn't recall all the details about their romantic entanglements.

"Were you at the party yesterday?" I asked.

"Yeah, but I wish I hadn't bothered," she said. "My date showed up with someone else and was drooling over her all night."

"Oh, ugh," I said. "You had a date, then? Was it through Hayley Sutton's blind dating service?"

"It was," she said. "Carey met Harris that way, I heard."

"She did?" Weird how her name kept cropping up. Or

maybe not, considering it was the only blind dating service in town and nobody seemed to be capable of sorting out their own problems. "When was this?"

"Hmm, a couple of weeks ago, when Hayley first opened her services to the public," she said.

We'd hired Harris to deliver Valentine's cards not much later. "Okay, thanks for letting me know. And thank you for the muffins."

I scooped up the bag and made my way back to the library. The sound of raised voices hit me the instant I opened the door.

Cass stood face to face with Cupid, her hands propped on her hips. "You're lying. I'm not an idiot."

"Cass, what are you doing?" Estelle hurried out of the corridor of our family's living quarters. "What's Tyler doing here?"

"I found him sneaking around the first floor," she said. "He claimed to be looking for you."

"I was!" he insisted. "She wasn't down here, and I assumed you wanted to know nobody was sitting at the desk."

"Weren't you meant to be watching the desk, Cass?" said Estelle.

"First I've heard," Cass said.

"I sent Jet to fetch you before I left for the bakery." I put down the bag of muffins on the desk. "Where is he?"

The little crow was good at hiding, but the absence of his usual chatter was noticeable. Worry washed over me, swiftly followed by alarm when I spotted his small winged body lying on the floor. I dropped to a crouch, relief flooding me when his beady eyes blinked open and he yawned.

"Did he fall asleep on duty?" said Cass, as Tyler looked on in bemusement.

I stroked Jet's feathers. "He's not under the effects of Poison Apple, is he?"

"He'd still be sleeping if he was," said Cass. "Nobody poisoned him. I won't let anything happen to your familiar."

I could believe that. Cass was more careful with animals than she was with people.

I gently lifted Jet back onto the desk. "Tired, are you? How'd you get glitter in your feathers?"

"This place is swimming in glitter," said Cass. "Even without the balloons. What do you want, then, Cupid?"

"Cass, that's enough," said Estelle.

There came a knock on the door from behind me. More to get away from their bickering than anything, I opened the door and found myself faced with Xavier. Biblio-witch or not, my capacity to go speechless around the Reaper was as reliable as Cass's temper. "Hey, Xavier. You don't have to knock during opening hours, you know."

He looked over my shoulder at the others. "Is this a bad time?"

A scrunched-up piece of paper hit me in the back of the head. I wheeled around and shot Cass a warning look, and she mouthed *go on.*

If she meant for me to start asking Xavier ridiculous questions about his boss in front of everyone, she could forget it. "Want to go for a walk?"

"You read my mind." Xavier took my arm, and I gladly went with him out of the library. "What's going on in there?"

"I made the mistake of taking a quick walk to the bakery," I said. "I forgot I can't leave my family members unattended without someone starting an argument."

"Your aunts aren't around?"

"Aunt Adelaide's tied up with the antidote," I said. "And Aunt Candace is chasing werewolves. As for Cupid, I thought he'd have the sense to stay at home until Hayley has stopped spreading rumours about us and accusing us of crashing her party."

"She blamed *you* for last night?" he asked. "Why? There were a lot of people wearing the same Cupid costume."

"Yes, and the arrows were fired while Tyler was talking to Hayley himself, so she knows he can't be responsible," I said. "But she still thinks Estelle of all people is plotting against her, and now she's accusing her of trying to ruin yesterday's event on purpose."

His eyes rounded. "She wasn't even there, was she?"

"No, but Hayley's lost all sense of reason, if she ever had any," I said. "I think only Aunt Candace had a good time last night, and she's completely out of her mind."

"Speaking of whom," said Xavier, "my boss found out about my visit to your family last night and gave me a long lecture about human courtship rituals being inappropriate for Reaper apprentices. If not for the incident at the town hall, I'd have been locked in all night."

My heart gave a lurch. "What did he say?"

Please say he didn't say we couldn't see one another. Please say he didn't go back on his word.

"He thinks spending too much time around humans is causing me to forget myself," he said.

Panic squeezed my chest. "I thought he said that before. He got over it."

"He didn't," said Xavier. "He's still watching to make sure I don't step out of line."

"He said you were more distracted when you weren't around me." My throat went dry. "Is… is that still true?"

"Why would you think otherwise?"

"Um." I faltered, tripping on the words. "I mean, because of what my aunt said the other day—"

He shook his head. "I don't blame you for what she said. Besides, I didn't *tell* him anything other than what he inferred himself. But I'm afraid he said I should decline all invitations to dinner with your family from now on."

The tight sensation in my chest loosened a little. "He's okay with the two of us dating, though?"

"As per your agreement—yes."

"Wait, this is about our agreement? He's taking it literally?" Was that a bad thing or a good thing? Well… that depended on how seriously the Grim Reaper took his promises.

"He wouldn't break his word, but that doesn't mean he can't interpret your agreement however he pleases," said Xavier. "And he was clear on one front—no more family dinners."

"You don't sound upset." A smile stole onto my face. "Believe me, I didn't think it would be that bad. I don't know why I didn't, considering Aunt Candace has been waiting for years for an opportunity to interrogate the Grim Reaper."

"You don't think I've never heard those questions before?" He took my hand and gave it a reassuring squeeze. "I don't blame you a bit."

"What about me being able to see Death?" I asked. "I'm not going to pressure you, but it's been bugging me lately."

His smile faded. "It has?"

"Yeah, but not because of you," I hastened to add. "I'm more worried that it points to something weird about *me*. I think the family I have is more than enough to deal with without adding secret Reaper relatives on top of them."

"You aren't a Reaper," he said. "It requires much more than seeing into Death to become someone like me. Besides, it's only been going on for the last month or so, hasn't it?"

A weight fell off my shoulders. "Not that I'd object to spending more time with you, but I think I prefer working for the library to running errands for the Grim Reaper. No offence."

"None taken." He glanced at the town hall across the square, and I followed his gaze. A few stray balloons drifted past, while glitter dusted the pavement outside. Otherwise, no traces remained of last night's events.

"Also, my Aunt Candace is still too smitten with that werewolf to think about flirting with your boss," I added. "Just to clarify. It's a nightmare-inducing mental image, I know."

"Lucky I don't dream, then." He grinned. "What else did I miss?"

"A fair bit." I told him all about my aunts' disastrous attempts at dating, starting with the mix-up at the blind dating service.

"Despite all that, Aunt Adelaide and the vampire she ended up paired with seemed to be getting on well last night," I finished. "Before the party broke up, anyway."

"I take it *her* date knew who she was?" he said.

"Of course he did," I said. "Who in their right mind would pretend to be Aunt Candace to get a guy?"

He chuckled. "That would be... entertaining."

"Or horrifying."

It felt good to laugh with him again, but when we passed the bakery, I couldn't help feeling a pang of guilt for how little progress I'd made at finding out who was truly responsible for shooting three people with poisoned arrows.

Xavier followed my gaze. "Zee's new apprentice was one of the victims?"

"Yeah, and it'll take another few days for the antidote to be finished," I said. "Since someone knocked over the cauldron."

"Who would do that?"

"No idea," I said. "Aunt Adelaide had to start the antidote from scratch because Aunt Candace is even more hopeless than usual this week."

"I wish I could help," he said. "Do you have any suspects?"

"Estelle's as confused as I am," I said. "Two of the people on our first list of suspects are out, now they've been shot, and we're left with three people in comas and a bunch of dissatisfied recipients of Valentine's cards. Oh, and Hayley, who thinks it's *our* fault."

"Did Hayley know your aunts were at the party?" he asked.

"She'd have seen them, but they weren't outside when the arrows were fired," I said. "I don't get where her accusations are coming from, except from jealousy. Estelle wasn't even there."

"Your new Cupid was."

"Yes, and he was talking to Hayley while the attacks happened," I said. "Pretty sure he can't be in two places at once. She just doesn't like us. Or rather, she doesn't like Estelle."

As we walked onto the seafront, my gaze drifted towards the police station. Had Edwin gained any new leads? It seemed unlikely, with all three people who might know the truth currently in comas and Mrs Jones breathing down his neck about the antidote.

"What is your aunt doing?" asked Xavier.

I followed his line of sight. *Oh, no.* Aunt Candace and Peter Barley stood on the pier. As we watched, the magnificent head of Cass's kelpie, Swift, rose from the rippling waves of the ocean.

"Look at him!" Aunt Candace reached out and stroked the kelpie's mane, ignoring his body language, which sat somewhere between annoyed and mildly murderous. "I told you he comes when you call his name."

"Cass is going to kill her," I said. "She hates anyone touching her kelpie without permission. Doesn't Aunt Candace know he's a wild animal?"

The kelpie leaned forward, shaking his head in a clear gesture telling her to go away.

Aunt Candace, however, had other ideas. She flicked her wand, causing the kelpie to rear back, and then bounded forward and swung her leg over the water horse's side.

I ran to intercept them, but I knew I'd never catch up in time. As I reached the pier, the kelpie leapt into the waves, and the two of them disappeared below the water.

11

"No!" I shouted, running along the pier, my feet striking the wet wooden beams. Xavier called my name, but I kept going, whipping out my Biblio-Witch Inventory.

Stabbing the page with a fingertip, I hit the word *rise*.

The kelpie lurched up out of the water, whinnying in distress. Aunt Candace hung grimly onto his mane, which made him lunge and kick harder.

"What are you doing?" Peter howled. "Now you've made it madder."

"I was aiming for my aunt!" I tapped the word again, but Aunt Candace clung on tighter, and the spell dragged both of them up in the air.

The kelpie shook his mane. Then he gave a tremendous leap, soared through the air and landed in the water with a splash that sent a wave soaring over our heads. As I raised my arms to shield my head—and my Biblio-Witch Inventory— Peter let out a remarkably wolf-like howl and dove off the pier into the water.

Catching my balance, I spat out a mouthful of salt-water and shook the pages of my Biblio-Witch Inventory, fervently grateful for the magic that stopped the ink from running when it got wet. Then my heart sank when I realised Aunt Candace had vanished below the surface of the ocean. *Where is she?*

A flash of a blond hair caught my eye as Xavier's head popped above the water. "Stay there, Rory!"

"You can't fetch both of them at once!" Alarm blared through me, and I frantically scanned the sea for any signs of movement.

Ripples on the surface drew my attention, and the kelpie's head broke through the waves, Aunt Candace still clinging to him like a life raft.

"Let go of the kelpie," I called to her. "I'll get you out."

"I'll do no such thing," she said. "I have no wish to drown."

"The kelpie doesn't want to get out of the water, and he's stronger than you are," I pointed out. "Let go and I'll pull you out."

"Not until I find Peter!"

"He's over here!" Xavier called from further out to sea. His blond head was barely visible above the waves, and a flicker of nerves stirred within me despite my knowledge that he couldn't drown.

"He's over there, Aunt Candace. Let go." I jabbed the word *rise* with a fingertip, putting everything I had into it, but Aunt Candace stubbornly refused to move. I needed to add something more. I grabbed my notebook and pen and wrote the word *amplify.*

The spell increased in intensity, breaking Aunt

Candace's grip. She flew upwards into the sky with a shriek. *Ah. Might've overdone it.*

"Hang on!" I scratched out the word, tapping on the page, and Aunt Candace crash-landed in a shivering heap on the pier.

"You," she said, "are going to pay for that."

Coming from someone who now resembled a red-haired swamp monster, those words sounded even more sinister than usual. Not that I looked much better myself.

"Peter!" Aunt Candace shrieked, running to the pier's edge as Xavier waded out of the ocean with Peter leaning on his shoulder.

Xavier led the werewolf to the beach, where he flopped onto one of the benches. "If I were you, I'd head home and warm up before you catch your death of cold. That means you, too, Candace."

Aunt Candace swooped down on him. "Don't you tell me what to do, Reaper. We had it under control."

"What the hell were you thinking?" I said. "Even you must know trying to ride a kelpie is suicidal at best."

"So is jumping into the sea, which *he* did." She jerked her head at Xavier.

"He doesn't need to breathe," I pointed out.

"And I suppose he can wrestle a kelpie single-handedly?" she grouched.

He *had* dragged the werewolf out of the water, and the guy was twice his size. Then again, I'd always suspected he must have supernatural strength to be able to carry a scythe strapped to his back every minute of every day. "It doesn't matter what he can do. Your sister *and* Cass are going to be furious with you when they find out what you did."

"Spoilsport." She sneezed. "Peter, are you okay?"

The werewolf coughed up a mouthful of water, looking blearily at her. "Yes, sweetheart."

I gagged behind my hand. Had he not seen that Aunt Candace's actions had got them into their near-death predicament to begin with?

"We're going home," I told Aunt Candace firmly. "Peter, can you walk?"

"I'll make sure he gets home," Xavier said. "You take care of your aunt."

"I will." I kept out my Biblio-Witch Inventory in case I needed to use it, but Aunt Candace marched towards the town square without looking back. So much for gratitude.

By the time we reached the library, I was shaking with cold and still pulling seaweed out of my pockets and hair.

Estelle gaped at the pair of us when we entered. "What in the world happened to you?"

I stayed beside the door in case Aunt Candace had a change of heart and decided to run back to Peter. "Aunt Candace decided to introduce her boyfriend to Cass's kelpie. Turns out he doesn't like being sat on."

"Of course he doesn't," said Estelle. "Why didn't you call for help?"

"Xavier helped," I said. "He's gone to take Peter home."

"I shall have to change my clothes," Aunt Candace announced. "Or else I'll catch my death of cold."

I rolled my eyes after her. "I don't understand what's the matter with her. Jumping on a kelpie's back is a bit extreme even for her. If Xavier hadn't been able to swim without needing to breathe, one of them might have drowned."

Estelle's gaze clouded. "I'll tell my mum. See if she can talk some sense into her."

As she walked after Aunt Candace, the door opened, and Xavier entered the library. Not a single droplet of seawater soaked his clothing, and he might never have set foot near the ocean at all.

"That was fast," I said. "You didn't take Peter home using Reaper speed, did you?"

"I know where the pack lives, so I gave him a push in the right direction," he answered. "I came back here because I was concerned your aunt might have taken off on you."

"She went upstairs to change." I should probably do the same, given that my teeth were chattering uncontrollably. "I'm sorry you were dragged into this."

"Don't apologise." He brushed a strand of damp hair from my face. Warmth sparked within me, chasing away the chill in my bones. "You should dry yourself off, Rory. I don't want you catching a cold."

"Wish you could give me a bit of that Reaper immunity." I drew my wand and gave it a wave to dry out my clothes. My cloak was still salt-sticky and uncomfortable, but I wanted to find out what was going on with Aunt Candace before I took a proper shower.

When Xavier left, I went looking for my family.

"What's *with* you?" Estelle was saying to Aunt Candace, who stood halfway up the stairs with her dripping cloak trailing behind her. "You're acting more erratic than usual, and that's saying a lot."

"I don't have time for these accusations," she said. "I'm going to change, and then I'm going to see Peter again."

"That does it." Aunt Adelaide entered the hallway and

aimed her wand at her sister. There was a flash of light, then Aunt Candace flopped over on her feet like a limp doll. Estelle caught her before she fell off the step, her own wand in her hand.

"Go on, bring her downstairs," Aunt Adelaide said impatiently. "It's time we found out what's wrong with her."

I pulled out my Biblio-Witch Inventory to help, and between the three of us, we levitated Aunt Candace into a kitchen chair. Aunt Adelaide got rid of the remaining seawater with a flick of her wand, then regarded her sister with her expression a mixture of concern and irritation.

"Is she under a spell?" Estelle said uncertainly.

"She's infatuated," said Aunt Adelaide, pursing her lips. "Judging by her behaviour."

"Only if Peter is, too," I added. "She nearly got both of them drowned and he was still smitten. Doesn't strike me as typical werewolf behaviour."

Estelle frowned. "Are you sure *she* didn't put a spell on *him?*"

"He wasn't even supposed to be her date in the first place." Aunt Adelaide waved her wand over her sister's head. "Estelle, can you watch the antidote while I run some tests?"

Estelle moved over to the stove. "Of course."

Aunt Adelaide continued to wave her wand and mutter under her breath for a few minutes, while I watched Aunt Candace in case she woke up and tried to make a run for it again. I couldn't believe I'd never wondered if she was under a spell before. Granted, her usual behaviour could be downright erratic when she was in pursuit of a research opportunity, but that didn't explain Peter's absurd overnight devotion to her, or hers to him.

"Are you sure she's the one who's under a spell?" I asked the others. "Estelle has a point—she might have spelled him."

"I'm reasonably confident my sister has never used a love charm in her life," said Aunt Adelaide. "Besides, the symptoms afflicting both of them do seem to mimic your average love spell. Infatuation, the demise of common sense..."

"And she didn't have much to spare to begin with." Werewolves couldn't use magic, not like witches or wizards could, so he couldn't have put a spell on her, surely.

Estelle turned away from the stove. "If it's a spell, when did it hit her? Not in the library."

"Maybe when they first met," I suggested. "Aunt Candace was acting normal before her first date, wasn't she? Apart from the bit where she ignored the fact that the names were mixed up, I mean."

Aunt Adelaide pursed her lips. "Being mistaken for me would have amused her even if no spell had been involved, but perhaps magic precipitated their initial affection."

"You mean someone sneaked up to them on their date and spelled them without being noticed?" I said.

"Or used a potion," said Estelle, giving the antidote a stir.

A love potion? Only a witch or wizard could cast spells... but anyone could buy a potion, even a werewolf. Still, Peter had been equally smitten with Aunt Candace, despite her deception.

"Nova Lyle was working on a love potion," I recalled. "But it kept blowing up in her face, and besides, that was after they had their first date. They went to a restaurant, right?"

"They did," said Aunt Adelaide. "However, they would have met at the town hall first and walked there together."

The town hall, where the blind dating service operated —and where the two latest victims had fallen under the effects of the Poison Apple. The same place where half the town had met their significant others, too.

Aunt Candace slipped in her seat, and I caught her arm before she fell headfirst onto the table and knocked over the bag of arrows.

"Have you checked these arrows yet?" I asked Aunt Adelaide.

"Which ones?" She indicated the two at the far end. "Those were spiked with Poison Apple, but we knew that already."

I lifted the bag I'd found in the Reading Corner. "These ones."

"I got distracted," said Estelle. "I checked one of them and it came up clean, but I'll get to the others when Aunt Candace is sorted out. Can the spell be reversed?"

"When I find out what it is," said Aunt Adelaide. "Can someone go and watch the front desk?"

"There's no need when there aren't any people visiting." Estelle gave the antidote another rigorous stir.

"Where'd Cass go?" I asked. "And Tyler?"

"I sent Cupid home," she said. "As for Cass, she must be upstairs. Don't tell her about the kelpie."

"I wasn't planning to." I walked out into the lobby. "Jet, are you here?"

"Here, partner!" He flew into view, his wings still dusted with glitter.

"Good," I said. "Is Cass around?"

"Yes, I am." Cass marched out from between the stacks. "What is everyone yelling about? And why's the floor all wet?"

"Aunt Candace," I said simply.

Her brows rose. "What did she do now?"

"Fell under a love spell, apparently," I said. "Did you see anything—"

"Did I see her acting weird?" she said. "Yes, I did, and I thought it was normal. I'm surprised anyone noticed."

"This was… more not-normal than usual." I'd consider telling her about the kelpie later, when she was in a better mood. "We need someone to watch the desk."

"I will, partner!" said Jet.

"You aren't going to fall asleep again?" I asked.

"It doesn't matter if he does, since nobody's here," said Cass. "This place is more of a ghost town than the Reaper's house."

"I doubt it," I said. "Everyone who was at the party is nursing hangovers."

"And grudges." She headed for the kitchen, where Aunt Candace remained in her chair. "What's up with her?"

"It's not a spell." Aunt Adelaide lowered her wand. "Not one that I can divine, anyway. If it's a potion, it'll wear off by itself."

"A love potion?" said Cass. "What, is that why she's smitten over that werewolf?"

"And he's infatuated with her in return," I added. "Are you certain it's a potion?"

Aunt Adelaide wasn't the type to jump to conclusions,

but considering her sister had been driving us all loopy for the past week, I didn't blame her for looking for a magical explanation. There was Peter's behaviour to consider, too.

"There's an easy fix," said Aunt Adelaide. "It's not hard to brew up an antidote for a love potion, even a powerful one. I'll get started on that, but I'll need the table."

"I'll move these." I picked up the bag of arrows, and a couple of them fell out of the hole in the bottom. "Oops."

Cass made no move to help me pick them up. "Is that the arrow the victim was shot with yesterday?"

"No, but those ones were." I waved a hand at the table to indicate the two arrows Edwin had given us. "These ones were abandoned in the Reading Corner."

I picked up the two which had fallen to the floor and nearly dropped them again when I saw the tips were bright pink.

Cass's brows rose. "Abandoned in the Reading Corner?"

"I don't..." I looked at the arrows on the table, then back at the ones in my hand. "These ones are spiked, too. I'm not sure if it's Poison Apple or not, though."

"What else would it be?" Cass interjected.

"Huh?" Estelle rotated on the spot. "The arrows you found in the Reading Corner were covered with potion, too?"

"Apparently." I gingerly held out the bag. "I thought you already checked some of them."

"I did, but not all of them." Estelle gave the antidote another stir, her expression darkening.

Aunt Adelaide swept over to my side. "You found

those arrows in the library? But you didn't see who put them there?"

"Cupid, of course," said Cass.

"No, I found them before he showed up," I said. "They appeared in the Reading Corner at some point overnight, or maybe yesterday. Either the person who owned them forgot they left them here…"

"Or someone wanted to frame us," Estelle finished. "Someone who's been in the library recently. But why would they do that?"

"I don't know, but this looks bad for us," I said. "Hayley already thinks we're guilty of sabotaging her party."

"She what?" said Cass. "Is *she* under a spell?"

"No, but she's had it in for me ever since I started organising this year's Valentine's-themed events," said Estelle. "I wouldn't put it past *her* to have arranged to have the arrows planted here. Who else would have a reason to frame us?"

"Maybe the culprit *wanted* Hayley to blame us," I said. "Or maybe they wanted to frame the students who use the Reading Corner. We don't know how long they were hidden there."

"I doubt it was an accident," said Estelle. "The first victim was our employee, and all the victims were shot with the same arrows we gave to our Cupid."

"Don't forget he's not the only Cupid in town," I reminded her. "I'm not saying it doesn't look suspicious, but it might be that the culprit decided this was a good place to dispose of the evidence without considering we might be blamed."

Cass made a sceptical noise. "How long were they hidden there? Did our first Cupid hide them?"

"You think he shot himself with one of his own arrows?" Estelle's forehead scrunched up. "No, that doesn't work at all."

"And he's been in the hospital with his overprotective mother ever since," I added. "Given where I found the arrows, I'd say one of the students put them there, but whether it was deliberate or not, I couldn't say."

"There's no way it wasn't," Estelle insisted. "Not with Hayley flinging blame at us for every little thing that goes wrong with her blind dating service. She's got a screw loose."

Aunt Adelaide cleared her throat. "Unless you want Candace to stay unconscious all day, I'm going to need help with brewing the antidote for the love spell. Can one of you fetch the ingredients?"

"I will," Estelle volunteered, and her mother took her place by the stove. I, meanwhile, picked up the rest of the arrows and returned them to the bag.

"What should I do with these?" I asked my aunt. "It's evidence, and unfortunately, it's more likely to be counted against us than against the person who put them there."

Estelle had a point... it did look like the arrows had been placed there to make us, or our Cupid, look guilty. Unless the culprit had simply used the library as a hiding place, but why risk the arrows being discovered?

"It's safe to say it wasn't Morris or Carey who put them there," I said. "They can't have shot themselves. Or each other. So... any idea who'd have a reason to shoot both of them?"

Cass snorted. "You think I know? Ask your Cupid."

"I would, if you hadn't chased him off," Estelle called from outside the kitchen.

"Hayley knows them both," I said. "But she seemed to genuinely think *we* were responsible for wrecking her party last night, and I don't see why she'd fake that. This seems like more than professional jealousy at work." To say the least.

"She knows most of the town," said Cass. "I think our so-called Heartbreaker Killer isn't as much of a criminal mastermind as everyone seems to think."

Aunt Candace let out a loud snore, drawing our attention back to her.

With a glance at her sister, Aunt Adelaide tutted. "Even if the arrows were left here by accident, it's still potential evidence. Keeping it out of the police's hands will only work against us."

Cass shrugged. "Do whatever you like. It'll be fine. Nobody thinks we did it."

Except Hayley.

Estelle returned to the kitchen, dumping a pile of ingredients on the table. "Are you brewing a generic antidote?"

"That was the plan," said Aunt Adelaide. "If it works, we'll have to contact the police and let them know. Not to mention Peter. If Candace is definitely under the effects of a love potion, there might well be other victims, too."

Estelle began arranging the ingredients she'd gathered on the table. "Might this be linked to some of the other incidents? People were angry with Harris for delivering cards to the wrong people, but if there was a love spell or potion involved as well..."

"You think Harris did it himself?" Or... hang on. What did most of the people who'd had an issue with Harris have in common? They'd used Hayley's blind dating services. "Don't forget most of the people who were at the party last night met their significant others in the same way."

"They signed up at the town hall," said Estelle. "Using Hayley's services."

"You think she spiked her customers' drinks with love potions?" Cass wanted to know. "Why?"

"To make her blind dating service seem successful?" I suggested.

Cass snorted. "Haven't you been talking about how much of a disaster this week has been for everyone's love lives?"

"I don't know, it was just a thought." Unless someone had wanted to ruin *her* business, making her blame us in the process—but why? I was still missing a clue somewhere, but perhaps the town hall might contain more evidence. Not that Hayley would be happy to see any of our faces within a ten-mile radius of her business. "Aunt Adelaide, what do you think?"

"I think my sister might be able to shed some light on the issue once she comes to her senses." She gave the antidote a stir. "Personally, I wouldn't say the arrows were planted here to pin the blame on us. They were too well-hidden."

"I can't believe you of all people think they weren't, Cass." Estelle conjured up a cauldron and began tossing ingredients into it. "You're usually the one who thinks people are conspiring against us. Whose fault do you think it is, then?"

"Whoever invented this Valentine's nonsense to begin with," said Cass. "Of course someone got mad and started shooting arrows at people. If you don't want my help, I'm going upstairs."

As she left the kitchen, Estelle continued to throw ingredients into the cauldron. "If they were under the effects of a love potion, they're not completely responsible for their decisions. Hayley saw to that."

"I wouldn't make accusations without proof." Aunt Adelaide cleared a space on the stove so Estelle could transfer her cauldron over there. "Also, are you making enough of the antidote for Peter, too?"

"I'll have some bottled and sent to him when it's brewed." Estelle joined her mother at the stove and gave her cauldron's contents a stir. "Sylvester or Jet can deliver it to him."

"I think Jet," I said. "I can't imagine anyone who just came out from under the effects of a spell would want to deal with Sylvester's teasing on top of realising they fell in love with Aunt Candace."

Estelle snorted. "Too true."

Aunt Candace herself still sat unconscious at the table. I couldn't deny that after all the trouble she'd caused this week, it was a marked improvement.

I'd never brewed an antidote before, but I passed Estelle ingredients for a few minutes while she stirred the antidote. "I hope Peter hasn't got himself into trouble. He doesn't even know he's under the effects of a love potion or spell."

"Which is probably the point." Estelle levitated the cauldron off the stove and onto the work surface at the side of the oven. "That ought to do the trick."

I passed her a vial, and she transferred some of the vivid blue antidote into it. Aunt Adelaide held out a hand for the vial. "I'll give it to her."

Estelle and I stood back as Aunt Adelaide carefully pushed her sister's mouth open and trickled three drops of the antidote onto Aunt Candace's tongue.

There was a long pause. Then Aunt Adelaide gave her wand a flick, and Aunt Candace's eyes opened. "As I was saying… where am I? And why am I covered in seaweed?"

"You jumped into the sea for a swim," I told her. "I had to fish you out, with Xavier's help."

"Interesting," she said. "The Reaper, you say? What did I do that for?"

"Do you not remember anything?" I frowned. "Peter? The kelpie?"

Her expression remained blank. "Who's Peter?"

"The man you went on a date with," said Aunt Adelaide. "The werewolf."

"Oh, yes, you were paired with him at the blind dating service," she said. "How did it go?"

Aunt Adelaide's mouth parted. Like the rest of us, she was lost for words. *She doesn't remember any of it?*

"There's no need to stare." Aunt Candace rose to her feet. "I think I'll go and change out of these clothes."

She left the kitchen, and I heard her climbing the stairs. Everyone remained silent for a moment.

"Did that just happen?" I asked. "How can she cause that level of chaos and not remember anything?"

"Maybe it's a side effect of the love potion," said Aunt Adelaide. "I can't say I'm an expert."

"How are we supposed to catch whoever did it to her if she doesn't even remember their first date?" said Estelle.

"It must have happened then," said Aunt Adelaide. "I'll wait until she's recovered before pouncing on her and asking questions, but there's no other time the potion could have been administered. She didn't even know who Peter was beforehand, and vice versa."

"Which means he can't have done it himself." But we knew that already.

"Do you want me to call Edwin and tell him what Hayley is doing?" asked Estelle. "She *must* have been the one who gave them both the potion. Nobody else has a motive."

"Without proof, Edwin wouldn't believe us," said Aunt Adelaide. "Given where you found those arrows, Rory, accusing Hayley might cause her to make a strong case against us in return."

"We need more eyewitness testimonies from other people who've used her services, then," I said. "We'll give the antidote to Peter, too, but half the students who were here in the library signed up to the blind dating service. If we question them again, we might find out who left those arrows behind, too."

Hayley? Maybe, but she must have an accomplice. And it still made no sense for her to sabotage her own party.

"Fine." Estelle conjured up a handful of vials. "I'll get the antidote ready."

12

The library was closed on Sundays, so I'd need to wait until the following morning to talk to the students. The blind dating service was open seven days a week, but I wasn't crazy about the idea of confronting Hayley without proof. Her accusations had seemed unhinged, to say the least, and it'd be worse if I marched in and started throwing accusations at her. Thankfully, the others agreed with me.

That left me one option for the following day... researching love potions, of which there seemed to be countless varieties. The antidote Estelle had brewed had been a generic one, and since Aunt Candace remained happily oblivious to her antics over the last week, Aunt Adelaide admitted she hadn't been able to identify the type of potion which had been used. No traces had been left behind, nor did there seem to be any logical reason why Aunt Candace wouldn't remember.

When Aunt Candace didn't come downstairs to breakfast, I decided to go looking for her. The room she dubbed her research cave was the obvious place to find her, so I climbed up the spiralling stairs until I came to the topmost floor.

I knocked on the door, and Aunt Candace answered a moment later. "Hello, Rory."

"Hi, Aunt Candace." Despite her obliviousness, I couldn't easily dismiss her stunt with the kelpie from my mind. Not to mention how she'd acted at our family dinner with Xavier. "Do you remember anything about the last week at all?"

"If you're referring to your attempt to introduce that Reaper of yours to the well-known pastime of being tormented by one's family members, then no, despite my sister's efforts to jog my memory," she said. "Would you consider inviting him over again so I can ask for a more accurate account of what I did?"

"No," I said. "I'm giving you the benefit of the doubt for now, but if you try making trouble with the Grim Reaper, I'll set Sylvester loose on your manuscript."

"There's no need to be so rude to an invalid," she said.

"You aren't an invalid," I said. "If you were, you wouldn't be walking around."

"I have supreme psychological trauma," she said dramatically.

"So does the poor kelpie."

She gave me a blank look. "Kelpie?"

I folded my arms. "Can you tell me the last thing you remember before Aunt Adelaide used the antidote on you? Do you remember meeting Peter at all?"

"Yes," she said. "I stayed here all night, thinking on the trauma of the last week…"

I suppressed an eye-roll, with difficulty. "How do you

know it was traumatic? For the rest of us, it was, but you seemed to be having the time of your life."

"The trauma is that I can't remember any of it," she said sourly. "Even my manuscript notes make no sense."

"Well, was Peter acting strangely when you first met?" I prompted. "Do you remember your date with him? You met at the town hall before going to the restaurant, right? Where did you go?"

"We went to the Gryphon's Tail," she said. "I had the steak. I remember ordering it, I think... unless it was a dream."

The restaurant was the most likely place for a love potion to be administered, but that was pure speculation. Perhaps Peter remembered more than she did, but who knew what his own mental state would be like after yesterday? I'd asked Jet to take him some of the antidote Estelle had brewed up, but we hadn't heard from the werewolf himself since Xavier had helped him home following his impromptu swim in the ocean.

"Let me know if you remember anything else," I said. "Have you spoken to Peter?"

"Why would I?" She leaned on the door frame, her expression mournful. "I can't recall a single second of our courtship. Such a waste."

Given that he spent most of the time thinking you were Aunt Adelaide, it's probably for the best.

Leaving her to her moping, I went downstairs and headed into the kitchen, where Aunt Adelaide had been up half the night watching the potion.

"Is she still playing the invalid?" she asked.

"Why not ask her to help you with the antidote to take

her mind off things?" I said. "It was her job, originally, even if she's forgotten all about it."

"I wanted to give her the chance to recover from her ordeal," she said. "And to remember where it started."

"She doesn't remember a thing," I said. "I'm having a hard time telling the difference between Aunt Candace normally and Aunt Candace under a spell, to be honest. I *think* someone gave her the love potion in the restaurant, but that's guesswork. Might Peter know?"

She rubbed her bloodshot eyes with the back of her hand. "According to that familiar of yours, he was in a foul temper after he drank the antidote."

"Jet said that?" I scanned the kitchen for my familiar, but the only thing on the table was a book of antidotes and potions. "What's this for?"

"When Estelle took over the antidote for a few hours last night, I researched love potions known to cause the drinker to lose their memory," she explained. "None of the potions in the basic guide fit the criteria. It'll be something more complicated, I don't doubt."

"I'll go and look." I had to do something useful, and I'd have more luck with the books than I would with Aunt Candace.

"If you like." She yawned. "If you're going to look up in the Potions and Poisons section, take Sylvester with you."

"All right." Estelle was sleeping in after a late night watching the antidote, so I walked across the ground floor alone. "Sylvester, I need assistance."

There was a long pause before the owl flew down to land beside me, at which point I'd already picked up the Book of Questions.

"Don't bring your Valentine's nonsense to me," he warned.

"The Valentine's theme is done," I said. "It's over. What's *not* over is the fact that three people are in comas and Aunt Candace just came out from under the influence of a love potion someone used on her illegally. Will the Forbidden Room give me the answers?"

"That's a question in itself, that is," he said.

"Oh, come on," I said. "That doesn't count. Will you please help me out?"

"Well, since you asked so nicely..." The owl landed in front of me. "What do you want to know about?"

"I just want to know where to start," I admitted. "Can the Forbidden Room identify a potion which was used on one of us?"

"No," he said. "Not if it didn't happen here in the library."

Worth a shot. "Okay, then I need help navigating the Potions and Poisons section."

He made a noise of disapproval. "How dull."

"Not if we find out what potion was used on Aunt Candace."

"There is no 'we'," said Sylvester, spreading his wings as though to take flight again. "I will help you if you agree to let me destroy those abominable balloons."

Seriously? Well, it wasn't as though we had another use for the balloons now the Valentine's poetry night was off. "One balloon."

"Two."

"Only if Estelle isn't around."

"Fine, then." He hooted. "We have ourselves a deal."

At least I'd done one thing right today. "All right, lead the way."

The owl flew up to the balcony, while I climbed the stairs to the Potions and Poisons Section. Love potions covered an entire row of shelves. It seemed witches and wizards had spent the last few centuries perfecting the art of bewitching the subjects of their affection.

"Don't touch that!" Sylvester squawked, as I pulled out a hardback book titled, *Infatuation Charms.*

"Why not—?" I broke off when the title page swam before my eyes, and a peculiar feeling came over me. Suddenly, the book was the most important thing in the universe. Nothing mattered more. Why were there other books on the shelves again? I reached out and knocked one of them to the floor. Those other books weren't worthy of sharing shelf space with this one.

Sylvester clipped me over the head with a wing, causing me to drop the book. At once, the spell broke, and I looked around in confusion.

"Ow!" I rubbed the side of my head. "What was that?"

"An infatuation charm." He clucked his beak. "Some of these books hold power in their pages."

"No kidding." I stepped back, while the owl picked up the textbook in his talons and returned it to the shelf. "Why doesn't it affect you?"

"I am already infatuated with myself," said the owl.

Figures. "Can you help me find a useful book, please? Preferably one which won't make me fall in love with it."

———

After a few frustrating hours reading up on complicated love potions, my phone buzzed with a message from Xavier.

Want to go for a walk?

Sure, I texted back, putting down the heavy book I was reading with relief. While I'd found a few books which weren't designed to bewitch anyone who read them, I'd come no closer to identifying the potion Aunt Candace had been given.

Sylvester, who was snoring loudly on a nearby shelf, opened his eyes when I stood up with the textbook tucked under my arm. "Are you done?"

"Not quite, but I need a break." I got to my feet, stretching out my neck. "Can you fly these books down to the front desk so I can look at them later?"

"You're full of demands today," he said. "One more balloon."

It seemed I'd discovered the secret to getting Sylvester to cooperate. "One more."

When I got downstairs, I found Xavier waiting for me by the desk. Sylvester flew past and dumped two textbooks on top of the desk, then flew back to get the rest.

"It's quiet out today." Xavier took my hand, and we walked outside together. "I take it we're not in danger of being shot by a stray arrow?"

"Not that I'm aware of, but I'm surprised Mrs Jones hasn't shown up again, considering how long the antidote is taking," I said. "I think we should avoid the police station, just in case any of the other victims have angry relatives waiting to pounce on us."

What with the new developments involving the love potion and the arrows, I'd all but forgotten two new victims were waiting for Aunt Adelaide to finish brewing the antidote.

"I didn't see anyone in the police station when I walked past earlier," he said. "Was your aunt okay after her swim yesterday?"

"Yes, but it turns out she was under the effects of a love potion the whole time," I said. "When Aunt Adelaide gave her an antidote, it wiped her memories of everything that happened over the last week."

His eyes sharpened with understanding. "She and Peter drank the same potion."

"You've got it," I said. "We're pretty sure it must have been during their first date. That would explain why Peter was irrationally infatuated with her even after she pretended to be her sister."

"Did Peter take an antidote, too?" he asked.

"Estelle sent him a dose," I said. "We haven't seen him since, so we don't know if he's suffering from the same weird amnesia effect as Aunt Candace is."

"Were there other victims?" he asked.

"I'd guess there were, but I wouldn't know who they are." I glanced across the square, where the town hall appeared as deserted as it had yesterday. "I've been looking up which love potions might have been used, but it'd have to be something easy to brew up."

"And hard to detect," he added. "You think this might connect to the issues you had with Cupid, too?"

"It's looking more and more likely," I said. "All the business with the Valentine's cards involved people cheating on their significant others or writing love notes to the wrong person. Or posting the cards without remembering doing it. Like Morris."

"He was one of the two victims on Friday," he said. "Do you think the person who shot Cupid might have blamed him?"

"It's as good a guess as any," I said. "Oh yeah—and we found more arrows hidden in the library."

"Which arrows?" he said.

"Arrows spiked with Poison Apple," I said. "I found them hidden in the Reading Corner. No clue who put them there."

"Speaking from an outsider's perspective, it sounds an awful lot like someone is trying to set you up," he said.

"Estelle thinks the same," I admitted. "She thinks it was Hayley. Cass disagrees and thinks she's innocent, but half the town has used her blind dating service and look at the havoc it's caused."

"That doesn't explain why she'd wreck her own party, though," he said. "Unless you think someone else shot the two victims. Not the person responsible for the love potion"

"That's the conclusion I'm leaning towards," I said. "If she used love potions to make her business seem like a success, she might not have predicted one of her clients would decide to play the part of a rogue Cupid."

As for her accusations towards us? They could be her trying to shift blame, or a guilty conscience. Who knew?

"I don't disagree, but you'll need proof," he said. "If your aunt doesn't remember, do you think any of the other victims will?"

"I'm not sure most of them even know they were under the effects of a potion…" I halted, spotting Nova Lyle emerging from the road which led to the town hall. Had she been meeting with Hayley?

"Rory?" said Xavier. "What is it?"

My gaze followed Nova. "That girl is an alchemist at the university, one of the few people who might have the skill to brew up Poison Apple. And... and she was working on a love potion, too."

"You think she was visiting Hayley and supplying her with love potions?" Xavier turned to the town hall. "If so, she might have left evidence behind."

"Are you volunteering to play detective?" I dropped my voice. "I doubt the Grim Reaper will appreciate you using your Reaper abilities to sneak around and spy on Hayley."

"What he doesn't know won't hurt him," he said. "You should wait outside, though."

"Wish you could use your Reaper powers on me." I could use another camouflage spell, but as a Reaper, Xavier could tread lightly and unseen, entering places nobody else could. Even a chameleon or invisibility spell wouldn't be half as effective. "Don't take too many unnecessary risks, okay?"

"I won't." He turned away, and then he was just... gone. I could see him out the corner of my eye, but not when I looked directly at him. *That's better than my chameleon spell.*

While I waited for him, I wandered up to the high street and found myself in front of the costume shop, *Dress to Enchant.* I'd never been there before, but maybe the owner would be able to shed some light on where the arrows I'd found in the library had come from. I might as well do something useful while I waited, so I ducked inside the shop and was swiftly surrounded by all manner of costumes, from ordinary pointed hats covered in flashing lights to spelled cloaks which changed one's appearance.

"Can I help you?" called the cheery witch at the counter. Her hair hung in ringlets, while her generous frame was cloaked in blue.

I walked up to the counter. "Do you have any more of those arrows left?"

"You're the first person who's asked me that today," she said. "Everyone else is trying to get rid of their arrows. I wouldn't have bothered selling them at a discount if I'd known everyone would try to return them the next day."

"They did?" I supposed they didn't want the bad memories hanging around. That, or they were all worried they'd be accused of being the rogue Cupid. "Okay. Thanks."

I hoped to find Xavier was back when I went outside, but no such luck. I wandered in the direction of the clock tower, debating using a chameleon spell so I'd look less like I was loitering—then I spotted a huge blond man crossing the square. Peter wore a murderous expression which intensified when he spotted me.

"You," he growled at me. "Come to have a laugh at me, have you?"

"Of course not," I replied. "I'm just waiting for a friend."

"Your aunt put a spell on me," he spat, without any of the good humour he'd shown when I'd seen him with Aunt Candace. "Then she tried to drown me in the ocean. I might not remember everything about the last week, but I remember that."

I backed up a step. "Aunt Candace was under the effects of a love potion, too. Someone wanted you two to be infatuated with one another."

"A likely story," he said. "She wouldn't even tell me her real name."

"We sent you the antidote as soon as we had one," I said. "I'm sorry Aunt Candace didn't tell you her real name, but the mix-up started with the blind dating service. Hayley's the person you want to talk to."

"She's in there?" He jerked his head at the town hall. "All right. Let's set the record straight."

"Wait!" I hurried after him, but the werewolf was much faster than I was, and the last thing I wanted was to draw Hayley's attention.

When the door of the town hall crashed shut behind him, I winced, wishing I'd waited for Xavier to return before speaking to the werewolf. It wasn't as though I'd known Peter would be wandering around in a temper, looking for someone to pick a fight with, but I really hoped Xavier had his Reaper skills turned up to max.

To my relief, Xavier himself walked into view a moment later. "Sorry. I had to get out. Peter was yelling at Hayley about putting him under a spell, and they were too close for me to risk staying any longer."

"Sorry," I said. "He was furious at me—or rather, at my aunt. I had to say something to stop him from marching into the library and starting a fight, but I didn't expect him to charge right in there and yell at her. Please tell me you at least found proof she was involved?"

"I'm afraid not," he said. "No love potions or anything else. No Poison Apple, either."

"Oh, no."

Not only did we have no proof, but if the werewolf mentioned I was the one who'd sent him in that direction, Hayley would have a real reason to hate my family.

13

"He didn't find proof?" Estelle stared at me. "Seriously?"

"None at all." I'd finished updating her on the latest, while she stood watch over the antidote on the kitchen stove. "Granted, he was interrupted when Peter barged in there and started yelling at Hayley. Who's going to tell Aunt Candace the bad news?"

"What bad news?" said Cass, entering the kitchen.

Estelle gave the antidote a stir. "That Peter the werewolf turned out to be a complete tool."

"Wasn't he under a spell?" said Cass. "Of course his real personality would turn out to be different."

"Yeah, but he got it into his head that Hayley is to blame without me even telling him she might have been responsible for the love potion," I said. "If she finds out I'm the one who sent him there, she'll have an even bigger excuse to get back at us."

"You only told him the truth when you said the love potion was probably given to him while he was on his first date with Aunt Candace," said Estelle. "It's clearly not our fault, not even Aunt Candace."

"I think we should let her know he's on the rampage, in case he shows up here demanding to speak to her," I said.

"It'll only upset her." Aunt Adelaide walked in. "Where did you run into Peter, Rory?"

"In the town square," I said. "On top of that, I saw Nova Lyle walking out of the town hall earlier. I thought she might be the one who's supplying Hayley with love potions, but they must have been well-hidden."

"Please tell me you didn't go snooping around," said Cass.

"Xavier did," I said. "He can use his Reaper abilities to make himself invisible, so he went into the town hall to look for evidence of any love potions. I really thought he'd find some."

Her brows shot up. "You sent him to spy for you?"

"He offered to," I replied. "But Peter interrupted by charging in to yell at Hayley before Xavier could search everywhere.

"Did he now?" Aunt Adelaide shook her head. "She has no reason to blame us if she didn't see you there, so I wouldn't worry about her."

"Assuming she hasn't heard about the arrows we found in the Reading Corner." Estelle wore a grim expression. "I have a headache. Can someone else take over?"

"What's got her in such a bad mood?" Cass asked as her sister left the kitchen.

"Someone *did* leave those arrows in the Reading Corner," I reminded her. "Which we still need to hand over to the police. Once Peter stops rampaging around looking for trouble, anyway."

"I imagine he'll be feeling as bewildered and angry as my sister is, for a time," said Aunt Adelaide.

"It was Aunt Candace he was mad at, but I'm not sure how much he remembers," I said. "He seems to think we pushed him into the sea on purpose."

"You never mentioned why he decided to go for a swim," said Cass.

Oh. Yeah. The kelpie. "It was more Aunt Candace's idea. Anyway, I didn't stick around to see how Hayley reacted to him yelling at her, in case she noticed me."

"If he comes here, he'll have to go through me first," said Aunt Adelaide. "I'll handle the antidote. Can you two check on the returns? Once they're dealt with, you can take the rest of the day off."

"There's a bunch of books on the front desk that aren't mine," said Cass. "Love potions, so I'm guessing one of you was looking them up."

"Oh yeah, Sylvester brought them downstairs for me." I walked out of the kitchen, followed by Cass. "I was trying to figure out what type of potion they used on Aunt Candace and why it's caused her to lose her memories. I'd have an easier time if Xavier had managed to find some evidence, but Hayley must have hidden it well."

"You really think she did it," said Cass.

I halted beside the front desk. "What, do you have any other ideas? Because I can't think of anyone else who'd have had any rational reason to put people under love spells. Even if it did backfire on her in a major way

"I can't believe she's still in business." Estelle walked

out of the stacks, rubbing her forehead, her eyes shadowed from lack of sleep.

"I didn't see anyone signing up for the blind dating service at the town hall earlier." Unless that was why Nova had been there, but she'd mentioned she wasn't interested in dating anyone. "Besides, you know how her party ended up. If I were her, I'd take a hiatus until everything has calmed down."

"At least she had a good turnout at her party." She leant against the front desk with a sigh. "I really thought the whole Cupid thing would be popular, but it's been a disaster from start to finish."

"We talked about not blaming yourself, right?" I asked. Then, in an attempt to cheer her up, I added, "That's usually my thing, not yours."

"She's not wrong," said Cass. "But if you're thinking of copying Hayley and running a blind dating service here in the library, I'm staying out of it."

"A blind date with a book isn't a bad idea," said Estelle. "But I think people are still too ticked off after the last week to want to go within a mile of any kind of dating service."

"That's it." Inspiration struck.

Cass snorted. "Really? A blind date with a book?"

"I don't see anything wrong with that idea," I said. "But there are other options."

"Such as…?"

"You're good at giving romantic advice," I told her. "If you ask me, more people need that than they need someone to deliver letters to the subjects of their affection."

"What, like an Agony Aunt thing?" she said.

"No thanks," said Cass.

"Remember Morris?" I said. "You gave him good advice. And if those letters have proved one thing, there's an awful lot of people in town who need assistance with disentangling their own problems before they even start dating anyone. Offer a free advice service, and... if you want to distribute the antidote to the love potion, that'll be the perfect time to do it."

Her brow furrowed. "You know, you might be onto something here. We'd have to make it confidential, though."

"And we're not in competition with anyone else, either," I added. "Hayley will have no reason to object."

"Assuming she doesn't show up and bring the police to arrest us," said Cass.

"Well, yes," I acknowledged. "But you know, it'll also be a good excuse to talk to the students again and figure out which of them might have been under the effects of the love potion, too. What do you think?"

———

We rose early the next morning to put our plan into action. Cass was her usual sceptical self, but Aunt Adelaide gave us the go-ahead to put up a poster on the front of the desk advertising the new Romantic Advice Service, complete with free drinks. Since we didn't know for sure who was under the love potion's effects and who wasn't, it was easier to distribute the cure to everyone who came into the library looking for romantic advice.

Estelle also repurposed Cupid's box with a label saying 'Poetry Night Confessions'.

"I thought that might be good for the people who are too shy to speak to the person they wronged face to face," said Estelle. "Anonymous confessions. We did a similar themed poetry night a few years back, where people wrote poems addressed to their person of choice, but without mentioning their names."

"So you want to go ahead with the themed poetry night after all, then?" I asked.

"Not the original theme, but a similar one," she replied. "As a bonus, since they're just poems, people can enjoy them for what they are, too."

"See, you're good at this," I said. "I'd never have thought of that."

Before long, patrons began to show up at the library. The first student to stop beside the box on the desk called Estelle's attention. "What's this?"

"We're doing a themed poetry night," she said. "We're also running a confidential romantic advice service. If you'd rather leave an anonymous note and get a reply in writing, we can do that, too."

"Are you sure it's anonymous?" asked one of the students.

"Absolutely," said Estelle, with an encouraging smile. "It's a trial run, but if it's popular enough, we'll make it a regular thing."

Over the course of the day, more and more people paused to look at the box, and by the end of the morning, we had a whole collection of anonymous love poems ready for the night. Tyler didn't show up—Estelle had opted to leave Cupid out of tonight's event to prevent any bad feelings from resurfacing—but several people asked after Harris and the others.

"The antidote will be done soon," I told them. "It won't be long until they're back on their feet."

Aunt Adelaide was still watching the antidote like a hawk, which left Estelle and me to deal with running the library for the day. Mostly me, because Estelle was buried in requests from students to help sort out their love lives. I ended up having to run the front desk more or less single-handedly. Which I wouldn't have minded, were it not for the fact that the person I suspected of brewing the love potion had yet to show her face.

Not that I'd expected her to. It wasn't until mid-afternoon that I had a spare minute to head up to campus to see Nova and ask what she'd been doing at the town hall yesterday.

"Are you sure you can manage?" I asked Estelle. "I can wait until we close for the day. Pretty sure Nova practically lives in the lab."

"I'll be fine," she said. "If you think she did it, it's best for us to find out before the poetry night. Just in case."

"Did you get any new information from any of the students you've spoken to so far?" I asked. "Any more clues about what kind of love potion they were given?"

"Nothing," she said. "Lots of contrite people begging me to tell them how to apologise to the people they wronged, but it's hard to prove who was under the effects of the love potion and who wasn't."

"Especially if they don't remember," I added. "I wonder if that's why some of them forgot they wrote notes for Cupid, or who they addressed them to."

I'd been dipping into the books I'd dug out of the love potions section yesterday whenever I had a moment to spare, but speaking directly to Nova would be the quickest way to see if she was responsible.

"If this Nova person did do it, I'm guessing she was working closely with Hayley," said Estelle. "Are you sure you want to go after her alone?"

"I'll take Jet with me," I said. "I'm not a hundred percent certain she knew what Hayley planned to do with the potion, though. She seemed more interested in the brewing process than actually *using* them."

Not that it made her any less guilty, if she'd been involved. The odds of this being a one-person job were slim, but even if Harris and the others woke up and revealed who'd shot them, that wouldn't explain who'd brewed the love potion. Not if it hadn't been the culprit's own doing.

Either way, if Nova could shed some light on the subject, it'd be more than welcome.

———

Jet rode on my shoulder to the lab, where I came to a halt outside the doors. "Jet, I need your help."

"What do you want me to do, partner?"

"Look around the lab for any signs of Poison Apple." I might not have made any headway on the love potion issue, but I'd memorised the main ingredients and told Jet. I just had to hope he'd remember them and wouldn't get distracted.

"Of course, partner!" He perched on my shoulder, ready to fly into the room.

Taking a deep breath, I knocked on the lab door. Then I opened it, finding Nova sitting in the same spot as before. Jet dropped from my shoulder and flew around the outskirts of the room, out of sight.

"Oh, it's you again." Nova flicked her wand to undo the earplug charm. "Rory, right?"

"That's me," I responded. "If you don't mind, I'd like to ask you a couple of questions."

"Oh?" She put down a jar of what looked like live eels. "About what?"

"Love potions." I spotted Jet flitting about in the background, but I did my best to keep my attention on her face. "Did you ever get anywhere with yours?"

"Love potions?" she echoed. "Oh, I gave up on them. I wanted more of a challenge. Why?"

"Someone's been spreading love potions among the town's citizens," I explained. "I have reason to believe it might be linked to Harris being shot. If the people he delivered letters to were under the effects of a love potion, then I need to find out what kind, and who gave it to them."

She blinked. "First I've heard. Who do you think drank the potion, then?"

"Morris Wilson, my Aunt Candace…"

Her expression was blank. "I don't even know those people. Should I?"

"Maybe not," I said, "but we suspect Hayley Sutton was involved in distributing the love potion. All the people who fell victim to the spell used her blind dating service."

"Really?" Her eyes rounded. "What… you think she did it? Why are you telling me?"

"You were seen at the town hall yesterday," I said. "And you're one of the few people on campus with access to the ingredients and the knowledge of how to brew a powerful love potion."

"I wasn't at the town hall," she said. "Who told you that? I went to run errands, and I stopped by to check on my friend at the costume shop, but I'm not interested in dating. I told you."

"Oh?" Maybe I'd misread the situation after all. "She mentioned everyone's returning the arrows."

"You talked to her, too?" she said. "What, you don't think *I* shot those people? I can't even pour a potion into a decanter without spilling it everywhere. As for the love potion, I told you, it blew up."

"True!" squeaked Jet, making Nova jump. "There is no love potion."

Nova looked at the crow, then back at me. "You sent your familiar to spy on me?"

"I sent him to look around the lab," I said. "You said anyone can use this room. Jet, did you find anything?"

Panic crossed Nova's expression. "Hang on…"

Jet flew over to me, gripping a folded-up piece of paper in his beak. I took the paper from him and gave it a scan. It might be covered in stains and old ingredients, but the title was unmistakable. *Poison Apple.*

Her shoulders slumped. "I didn't plan to use it. It was a practise run for my advance poisons module."

My brows shot up. "You *did* brew the Poison Apple? Where is it?"

"I don't know," she said. "I thought I'd misplaced it somewhere in here, before I heard Harris was shot. That's why I was visiting Lee at *Dress to Enchant*—I hoped she might remember who bought the arrows, but she sold the exact same costume to two dozen people."

"What, you're saying someone stole the Poison Apple out of the lab?"

"You're welcome to look for it." She looked down at the potion-stained desk. "I wasn't kidding when I said I don't usually keep an eye on whoever comes in and out of this room. It might have been anyone."

Anyone at the university, at least. "What about the love potion?"

"There's no love potion," she said. "It's near-impossible to brew one with a consistent effect. How many people are affected?"

"I couldn't say," I said. "It either happened while they were at the town hall or while they were on their dates."

"Must have taken some serious organisation, if it's true," she said. "Everyone who used the blind dating service went to different places, from what I heard."

Good point. Was that why not everyone had been affected? "I don't know about organised. It feels random." Like the perpetrator hadn't cared how much trouble they'd caused. "Anyway, do you have an antidote for the Poison Apple?"

"No, because I never planned to use it," she said. "Isn't your aunt brewing one?"

"Yes, but someone knocked over the first dose." Still, we'd almost made up for lost time by now. And Nova hadn't been in the library when the antidote had been knocked over. Which put me back at square one again.

"Bummer," she said. "I can't help with that, but I can brew up a love potion antidote."

"We're working on it, but thanks," I said. "Oh yeah—do you know of any love potions which come with amnesia as a side effect?"

"Amnesia?" she echoed. "No… not off the top of my head, anyway. Don't you have books on that in the library?"

"We do," I said. "Thanks anyway."

Jet flew onto my shoulder as I left the lab, and I gave his feathers a stroke. "What's up, partner?"

"I'm still lost," I admitted. "Someone sneaked into the lab and stole the Poison Apple without being noticed. I know when the victims wake up, we'll know who did it, but I'm not sure that will be the end of it. As for the love potion…"

It wasn't Nova. Then who had been responsible? If even she hadn't known of any potions with amnesia as a side effect, was it even a potion at all?

14

I headed back to the library, turning the information over in my head. Nova had made the Poison Apple, and it must have been another student who'd stolen it to use against Harris, because they blamed him for the magical mayhem ensuing from whoever had used the love potion. As for Carey and Morris, they'd both been victims of the prankster's antics as much as Harris himself had.

Estelle wore a brighter expression than I'd seen on her in a long time when I opened the library doors. "We're getting dozens of signups for tonight," she said. "Any luck?"

"Nova is the one who brewed the Poison Apple," I told her. "She claims someone stole it from her and used it against Harris. But she doesn't have a clue about the love potion. When I saw her yesterday, she was visiting her friend at the costume shop, not the town hall."

Her smile faded. "How do you know she's telling the truth?"

"She seemed genuinely confused about the whole

thing," I said. "She also volunteered to hand out an antidote to anyone affected at the university."

"Maybe she's covering her tracks," she said. "She brewed the Poison Apple but not the love potion?"

"The love potion blew up in her face," I said. "Anyway, she pointed out that all the people who used the blind dating service were at different places when they were on their first dates. So unless the person responsible was at every pub or restaurant in town at the same time..."

"Then they did it at the town hall," Estelle said.

"Not if it was a potion," I reminded her. "Also, it didn't affect everyone. Maybe only certain restaurants or pubs were affected. I didn't see anything weird at the Black Dog when Xavier and I went there."

Her brow crinkled. "Nobody's ever actually seen the perpetrator, have they?"

"I guess not," I said. "Maybe they used a camouflage spell."

"Seems as good a guess as any," she murmured. "Maybe it *was* Hayley herself. Or she has another employee."

"Isn't she more or less running the whole operation alone?" I said. "That's the impression I got. And I'm still none the wiser as to who stole the Poison Apple and used it to shoot people as Cupid."

Sylvester landed on the pile of books in a swoop of wings. "Isn't this a conundrum?"

"Do you have any better ideas?" I asked the owl. "I've been looking in those books you helped me find, but none of the potions come with amnesia as a listed side effect. Nova couldn't think of any, either."

"That's because there aren't any."

"You're telling me this now?" I looked between the owl

and Estelle, more perplexed than ever. "I thought you knew everything."

He released a hooting noise with a threatening note as though warning me not to give his secret away in front of Estelle. "Not all at once. Even a genius such as I."

I gave a snort, though I recalled him saying something similar once before. He might be all-knowing, but he'd told me the knowledge of the Room of Questions mostly stayed locked inside said room. He'd had overnight to fly into the room and look around for information, but it was rare for him to bother without being asked directly by one of us.

"What?" said Estelle. "Sylvester, what do you know."

"A great many things." He shuffled his feathers in a self-important manner. "It seems we have someone who is capable of using love spells on people without being seen, sensed or heard, even by the most observant of individuals."

"Did they use a camouflage spell, then?" I asked. "You do think they used a spell and not a potion? I thought we ruled out love spells."

"What makes you think the perpetrator was human?"

I frowned. "Excuse me? Are you confessing?"

I was only half joking. I could see Sylvester thinking it was funny to mess with Aunt Candace, but I couldn't picture him putting people under love spells all over town for his own amusement. Besides, he had little power outside of the library.

"Of course not," he said. "I have much better things to do with my time."

No, but if the culprit was around his size and had wings, it would explain how they'd got around without being traced. "Someone has a familiar who can turn invisible?"

Estelle's eyes flew wide. "Was it them who hid the arrows in the library? And knocked over the antidote?"

"That doesn't explain who the mastermind was," I said. "Familiars can't cast spells, can they?"

"No, but it's a start," said Estelle. "Maybe I can jog Aunt Candace's memory—"

The door slammed open and Edwin strode into the library. "Where is that Cupid of yours?" he demanded.

"Who, Tyler?" said Estelle. "At home. Why?"

"The letter!" he said. "That Cupid gave the letter to the wrong person! I also received a number of calls from Hayley Sutton accusing you of sabotaging her business."

"Whoa." I took a step away from the furious elf policeman. "Tyler's no longer working for us. Also, Hayley's been making accusations with no proof ever since she found out we were hosting Valentine's Day events at the library."

"She claimed you were responsible for shooting two of her guests," he said. "On top of that, Karen doesn't know I exist. She never got my letter."

"Karen?" Estelle echoed. "Are you sure that's who you wanted to deliver a letter to? Your ex-girlfriend showed up here the other day and she was very upset."

Is he under the spell, too? Maybe I should have asked Nova to brew an antidote for the whole town.

"There's no ex-girlfriend." His face went beet red. "This is an outrage."

"Come and tell me all about it," Estelle said. "I'm offering an anonymous advice service."

I stepped in. "And if you'd like to talk to my aunt about

Hayley, you're welcome to come with me, but she can't leave the kitchen at the moment."

Estelle caught my eye, frowning in confusion. Then when I mouthed, *he's under the love spell,* she gave a nod of understanding. "Come with us, Edwin."

The elf tottered after us, muttering under his breath, until we reached the kitchen.

"Oh, hello, Edwin," said Aunt Adelaide, with some surprise. "Can I help you?"

Estelle mouthed, *he's under the love spell* at her, then said to Edwin, "Why not take a seat? My mum will take care of you."

While the bewildered elf sat down, Aunt Adelaide picked up a vial from the sideboard. I stood in front of Edwin's view while she passed it to Estelle.

"Do you remember when you decided to deliver Karen Thompson a note?" I asked the elf.

"Karen?" he echoed. "Always. I always loved her."

Behind his back, Estelle conjured up a glass of liquid and surreptitiously slipped the antidote into it. "Care for a drink, Edwin?"

"I don't think—" He reluctantly took the glass from her.

"I insist," added Aunt Adelaide. "I'll have one myself."

She conjured a glass of her own—without the antidote—and drank deeply. With a confused blink, Edwin did likewise. "I always loved... Karen..." He trailed off, his eyes sliding closed.

"That'll do it," Aunt Adelaide murmured.

The elf's eyes opened again. "What is going on?"

"You were under a spell," said Estelle.

He shook his head. "What have you done to me?"

"It's just an antidote, but you'll be feeling disorientated for a while," Estelle said soothingly. "Um, also, how do you feel about Karen Thompson?"

"Who?" he said. "Are you making fun of me?"

"No," Aunt Adelaide interjected. "You just came here telling us how much you love Karen."

The elf policeman shook his head again. "Must have been a late night... what did I say?"

He doesn't remember. The amnesia must have kicked in.

"You were under a spell," Estelle said, in a firmer voice this time. "Someone made you fall in love with Karen Thompson."

"Karen?" he said. "I've never spoken to her in my life."

"I'm afraid that isn't true," I said apologetically. "Someone in town has been putting love spells on people. Did you meet Karen through the blind dating service, by any chance?"

"No." He gave another head-shake. "A love spell, you say? What day is it?"

"Valentine's Day," said Estelle. "Were you dating a blond woman?"

"Flora?" His face fell. "We broke up last week. Poor Flora. She doesn't know about... about this love spell, does she?"

"I'm afraid she does," said Estelle. "If you'd like to apologise to her, we're running a themed poetry night..."

She escorted the elf policeman out of the kitchen, while I remained behind, more confused than ever. "He *didn't* use the blind dating service?"

"Apparently not," said Aunt Adelaide. "I'm inclined to think the poor man was telling the truth."

"Oh, we forgot to give him the arrows," I said, seeing the bag lying on a chair.

"Did he look like he was in any fit state to handle spelled arrows?" said Aunt Adelaide. "No… we're better off waiting until Harris and the others wake up. It'll only be a few hours."

"Good," I said. "Speaking of antidotes, I think we'll need more of the one for the love spell than I thought."

Question was, if not the blind dating service, then who might have kicked off the whole thing? It seemed more of a practical joke than anything malicious, unless the person responsible was a misanthrope who wanted to ruin everyone's love lives.

I walked out of the kitchen and spotted Estelle escorting Edwin to a side room, no doubt to give him advice on how to mend things with Flora. I halted at the front desk and picked up the topmost book on the pile of guides to love potions. "There's no pattern to this. He didn't use the blind dating service. Whoever is doing this doesn't seem to care who they target."

Sylvester landed on the desk next to the books. "I don't know why I bother with you people sometimes."

"You said it wasn't a human who was responsible," I said. "Care to elaborate on that?"

"No, I thought I'd let you figure it out for yourself." He took flight, knocking over the pile of books. They fell to the floor in a heap.

"Really." I crouched to pick them up. The first textbook lay open at the index, and the name *Cupid's Arrow* stood out on the page. "There's a potion called *Cupid's Arrow?*"

Forgetting the other books, I grabbed the basic guidebook to love spells and flipped forward to the right entry. *Cupid's Arrow, a powerful love potion based on the spells cast by pixies and other fairies, which formed the basis for the modern love spell.*

Fairies. I skimmed pages until I came to the glossary. *Fairies. Little known, compared to other beings. Can use glamour to trick and beguile.*

My head jerked upright. "Sylvester, can you fetch me a basic guide to fairies? I think I've got this."

———

Sylvester returned with the book without making a fuss, for a wonder. One scan of the opening chapter confirmed my theory. *Fairies can use a type of magic called glamour to make themselves invisible to sight. They can also use glamour to enthral mortals and produce an effect like infatuation, and cause humans to lose track of time and otherwise forget their responsibilities.*

The sound of a door closing made me look up. Estelle was back, and Edwin must have just left. "Poor Edwin. He asked me for advice on fixing things with Flora, but since he doesn't remember most of the last week, it's anyone's guess as to whether he'll be able to use it or not."

"He's gone, then?" I tucked the book underneath my arm and carried it into the kitchen. "Did he believe you?"

"I think he did." Estelle walked into the kitchen behind me. "But considering how dodgy his memory is at the moment, he can't tell fact from fiction."

"I guess not." I laid the textbook down on the table. "Did you warn him about Mrs Jones calling the police every hour to yell at them about the antidote?"

"With any luck, that won't be an issue anymore by tomorrow," she said. "As for Hayley… you know, I don't think she did this, not anymore. Whoever spread around this love spell didn't care how much damage they did."

"We're looking for someone who just wants to wreak havoc," I said. "None of the suspects fit that criteria."

"Even Aunt Candace," said Aunt Adelaide. "Why, do you have a theory, Rory?"

I lifted the textbook and opened it on the introduction. "What's small, winged, a notorious prankster, can turn invisible, and can also use glamour to cast a love spell on someone?"

Aunt Adelaide spun around so fast she nearly knocked the cauldron off the stove. "Pixie wings!"

"Excuse me?" said Estelle.

Aunt Adelaide lifted the jar of pixie wings into the air. "The origin of Cupid… no wonder it was drawn to town, with everyone wearing costumes."

Estelle looked between us. "What in the world are you two talking about?"

I held up the book. "The person behind this isn't human. Sylvester was right."

"I've been waiting all year to hear that." Sylvester flew into the kitchen and dropped two more textbooks on the table. "You're welcome."

"Fairies." Estelle clapped a hand to her mouth. "You think a *fairy* did this?"

"A pixie." I'd met lots of shifters, vampires, witches and other paranormals, but fairies weren't something I knew much about at all. But just reading the introduction to the guidebook had made more sense of the recent events than anything else. "They can turn invisible, move around without being seen, *and* cast infatuation charms. They also leave glitter everywhere they fly. You know we've been finding it everywhere in the library…"

Estelle shook her head. "And to think Cass blamed the glitter on the third floor on my balloons."

"Hayley must have thought we were sabotaging her because she couldn't see who was spelling people," I added. "And we thought she was acting in retaliation, but it was someone else—someone invisible. Switching out the notes in the box of Valentine's cards, making people fall in love at random… even planting the arrows here."

"Not that," said Estelle. "Pixies are placid and friendly creatures, by reputation. Not violent or malicious."

"There must be a human influencing the pixie's actions," said Aunt Adelaide. "Pixies can pick and choose who they show themselves to, and it's not unheard of for them to befriend a human if they come to trust them."

"I bet the pixie stole the Poison Apple from the lab, too," I added. "It wasn't just Nova being unobservant."

"You're right," said Estelle. "But… how are we supposed to catch something that's invisible?"

I turned the page. "That's why I have this."

15

After discussing the plan with the others, I walked out into the lobby. There was so much glitter everywhere that it was beyond me to figure out if the pixie was inside the library or not. For all we knew, it'd been hiding underneath our noses the whole time.

Sylvester perched on the front desk, giving an impatient flap of his wings. "Aren't you going to thank me for leading you to the truth?"

"I already did," I said. "Sylvester, what advice would you give us for trapping a pixie?"

"Read that book of yours," he said. "I doubt a pixie will come within sniffing distance if you leave a jar of dead pixie wings on display."

"Ah," said Estelle. "Yeah, I'll tell my mum to put those away."

Estelle ran back to the kitchen, while I continued to skim through the book. Pictures of small winged creatures filled the pages. Pixie wings. Like Cupid.

There came a loud crash from somewhere above, and I ran to the stairs. "Cass, are you okay?"

No response came. My heartbeat kicked into gear. I didn't see any pixies, but then again, I wouldn't, not if the pixie didn't want me to see it.

Cupid's arrows…

"Cass?" I began to climb the stairs. "I'm coming upstairs."

"Stop right there," said a harsh voice.

I halted beneath the stairs. Tyler appeared on the balcony, leaning over with his crossbow pointing right at me.

So it was you. "There's no point in shooting me," I said, trying to keep my tone even. "The antidote's almost done."

His hands trembled on the crossbow. "I won't let you take my pixie away."

Cupid. Tyler had worked for Hayley… and he'd certainly have good reason to sabotage her blind dating business. And while not everything had gone as planned, according to what I'd read so far, pixies were notorious agents of chaos and difficult to control.

"Why'd you do it, then?" My hand crept closer to my pocket and my Biblio-Witch Inventory, but the lack of any signs of his invisible companion made me wary.

"I didn't want things to get this far out of hand," he said. "It was just a laugh at first, switching the letters around, zapping people with love spells."

"Was that why you shot Harris?" I asked. "Because that wasn't much of a joke. You let him take the blame, too."

His face crumpled. "He didn't deserve Carey."

"Carey?" I blinked. "You like Carey? She was shot, too."

"An accident," he said. "I asked him—the pixie—to

throw arrows around at random during the party so it would seem obvious I wasn't involved."

"That's why you went?" I said. "Why'd you go inside to talk to Hayley, then?"

"So she saw me, of course." He squared his shoulders defiantly.

"You really didn't think this through, did you?" Estelle said from behind me. "And stop pointing that thing at Rory."

He bared his teeth and fired off a wild shot with the crossbow. I retreated downstairs, pulling out my Biblio-Witch Inventory and hitting the word *Rise*. Tyler rose into the air with a shriek, flipping upside-down and struggling to keep hold of the crossbow. "Don't hurt me!"

"Put the crossbow down," Estelle said. "I can't believe you lied to my face when you said you wanted the job."

"I did want the job." He rotated on the spot, his face turning purple. "If you hadn't taken responsibility for brewing the antidote, I'd have left your family out of this."

"You shot my employee and then took his job," Estelle said, her face flushed with anger. "And you knocked over the antidote on purpose to delay the inevitable moment when he told us it was you."

"Don't forget how he got his pixie to hide the arrows inside the Reading Corner, so that we'd take the blame," I added.

"Not you," he gasped out. "I didn't know where else to put the rest of the potion, so I hid it on the arrows. It didn't matter who found them."

"You even got your pixie to put Jet to sleep, didn't you?" I said. "And Sylvester."

"I didn't harm anyone," he insisted. "If I hadn't hired

Spark, he'd have flown around town creating chaos anyway. I just gave him something to do."

"You made a lot of people unhappy," said Estelle. "You ruined Hayley's party and nearly put both of us out of business."

"Hayley deserved it," he said. "You weren't supposed to end up involved."

"Even if you ignore what you did to the library, you bewitched my aunt and nearly caused her and Peter to drown in the ocean," I added. "Not to mention hurt Cass's kelpie."

"You did *what* to my kelpie?" Cass appeared on the balcony above Tyler, a murderous expression on her face. "Oh, you're in for it now."

Glitter flashed in the corner of my eye, and a small winged creature appeared at my shoulder, his hands glowing with purple light. About eight inches tall, he had pointed ears and tufty blond hair, while his clothes were the colour of bark.

"Sparks protects me," said Tyler "If you harm me, he'll bewitch you. He can make you forget all about your feelings for the Reaper altogether if I ask him to."

My hands clenched. I spotted a pair of tawny wings out of the corner of my eye and gave a faint nod. "That's none of your business. Besides, you aren't the only one in here with a winged assistant."

A deafening *bang* sounded from above, and the pixie took flight with a shriek, only to collide with a shower of confetti. The sound of a dozen balloons bursting echoed like fireworks as Sylvester and Jet flew in circles, balloons shredded beneath their wings and claws, sending confetti and glitter raining down on our heads.

Tyler yelped and dropped the crossbow. Cass ran downstairs and caught it, pointing an arrow at his chest. Tyler whimpered. "Please don't."

"You shouldn't have messed with the library!" Estelle shouted, casting a spell that bound Tyler's hands and feet.

When she levitated him to the ground, he stopped struggling, collapsing into a pile of confetti. Sylvester, meanwhile, caught the struggling pixie in an outstretched claw. "I still get to destroy two more balloons later?"

I rolled my eyes. "If it means that much to you."

16

Two hours before the poetry night was due to start, we found ourselves at the police station. Tyler and his little friend had been hauled away to the jail, and while Edwin remained a little disorientated after his loss of memory following the removal of the love charm, he was all too happy to have Tyler put behind bars. We were lucky the generic antidote worked on pixie charms as well as potions.

With Estelle in charge of the library and Cass backing her up, Aunt Adelaide strong-armed Aunt Candace into delivering the antidote for the Poison Apple to Harris and the others at the hospital, as well as promising to speak to Peter at the next opportunity.

"Tyler will pay a hefty price for his crimes," said Edwin. "However, there is the matter of the pixie. We've never arrested one of his kind before, and he's already escaped his cell twice."

"Have you asked him for an explanation for why he decided to break the law?" asked Aunt Adelaide.

"The pixie doesn't seem to speak English," said the elf. "However, he did demonstrate remorse for the trouble he caused. The problem is, there's no laws covering what he did while he was obeying Tyler's commands, and locking him in jail would be like arresting someone's familiar. There's no standard rule dictating the average sentence for a pixie."

"You can't be saying you're going to let him go," said Aunt Adelaide.

"Pixies are simple creatures," he said. "He'll likely obey the next person to take him in, assuming he doesn't leave town altogether."

"All right," I said. "Tyler is the one who deserves a jail sentence."

"Yes, he does," said Aunt Adelaide. "Very well, you're welcome to let the pixie go, provided he behaves himself this time."

Edwin nodded to his troll guard, who shuffled through the door at the back of the reception area leading to the jail cells. He returned a minute later with the pixie fluttering at his side.

"I can't understand a word he says and I'm not sure he understands me either, but he has enough of a command of the English language to know when he's being given orders," Edwin said. "He answers to his name, too, Spark."

At that, the pixie jumped to attention, his small wings beating as he hovered on the spot. The trolls didn't look happy, grumbling and squinting suspiciously at him. Given the new layer of glitter on the floor, I could guess why.

"It makes sense that he'd have picked up some of our language, if he's been living around humans for a while."

He was cute, really, a little winged creature who some-what resembled a stick insect with wings. Not really what I'd associate with the word 'fairy', but imagining him with a bow and arrow in his hands went a long way to explaining why the magical world had used him as a model for their Cupid.

"Nobody knows where he came from, but I'm sure he has a home to go back to." Edwin nodded. "Spark? You can leave."

At once, the pixie vanished in a puff of glitter.

"We'd better get moving," said Aunt Adelaide. "We don't want to miss the poetry night."

"You're still hosting an event tonight?" asked Edwin.

"The poetry night has a theme tonight—anonymous love confessions and apologies," I explained. "We thought it might help clear up some of the bad feelings this week's events have brought on. Half the town's coming."

"If that's the case, then I may see you there later," he said. "I believe that's your sister waiting outside."

Sure enough, Aunt Candace accosted us at the doors. "Is it over? Have the guilty been punished?"

"Provided nobody else gets any ideas," I said, as we headed back towards the library. "The whole town will know about the pixie soon enough."

"I doubt he'll risk showing himself in front of humans again," said Aunt Adelaide. "Candace, did you deliver the antidote to the hospital as promised?"

"Of course I did," she said. "They were very grateful for it."

"Even Mrs Jones?" I arched a brow.

"Funny thing, that," she said. "Shortly before the anti-dote was administered, someone thought it was amusing to burst several balloons outside Harris's room. The boy slept through the whole thing, but I heard there was quite a stir. Seems that Mrs Jones is terrified of balloons."

Sylvester. I should have known.

"Imagine that," said Aunt Adelaide. "He'd better not do the same at the poetry night. Are you going to be there, Candace?"

"I think I'll pass," said Aunt Candace.

"What about you and Peter, though?" I asked. "Going to write him a poem?"

"Poetry," she said, "is *not* my area of expertise. Besides, he knows I was under the influence of a spell."

"Not all the time," said Aunt Adelaide. "The pixie wasn't responsible for your not telling him your real name."

"Why, I quite literally wasn't myself." Aunt Candace put on a wounded expression. "He knows the truth, the spell is gone, and there's no harm done."

"Except for one mildly traumatised kelpie," I said. "I'm surprised Cass didn't react worse than she did. We'll probably get back to the library to find she's turned your manuscript into a kumquat."

"What's life without a little unpredictability?"

Honestly.

"What about the vampire?" she added to her sister. "Are the two of you going to the poetry night together?"

"Oh, no," Aunt Adelaide said. "We already decided to put this behind us and move on. Have a fresh start. Sometimes that's the best option."

We arrived back in the library to find the poetry night already kicking off. There was a big cheer from the gathering crowd when Estelle announced that the antidote had been finished and Harris and the others would wake up soon.

Then came the poems themselves. Everyone who took part picked a poem at random from the box, some of whose recipients were easy to guess, others not so much. A fair few people guessed which poem was Harris's passionate apology to both Carey Langdon and Laila Chen, while Morris had words to say to apologise to both Maura and Liz. Edwin showed up halfway through the night, looking a little tired, but he slipped his own poem into the box, and sat at the back, occasionally glancing at the blond woman in front of him with a mournful expression on his face.

The poetry night continued until almost eleven o'clock at night, and not a single fight broke out. As the evening finally drew to an end, the poetry night's participants began to file out of the library. I even spotted Peter and Aunt Candace talking in whispers, the latter's notebook and pen nowhere in sight.

"At this rate, I'll need to hire an assistant to help me out next week," Estelle whispered to me. "I think I'll go without the Cupid costume this time, though."

"Yeah." I smiled. "I think this is the most popular poetry evening we've had. Glad you didn't cancel it."

Hayley was notably absent, but since it was clear neither she nor Estelle had been responsible for the other's misfortune, maybe the two of them would be able to make up with one another once the sting of recent events had faded.

"Yes, well done." Cass walked towards us. "Someone else sneaked in, too."

She held out a hand, and the pixie blinked up at us

from her palm. His tiny wings beat as he flew over to Estelle, making inquisitive noises.

"I should have guessed he'd find his way to you, Cass," I said.

"Actually, I found him sitting on the front desk by himself," said Cass. "What were you saying about needing an assistant?"

Estelle looked between her and the pixie. "Please tell me you're joking."

The pixie flitted over to Estelle and flew around her head before perching on her shoulder.

"Well, well," said Aunt Candace. "If I didn't know better, I'd say someone wants to apologise."

"What about you?" I spotted Peter crossing the lobby to the exit. "Did you two clear things up?"

"Crystal clear." She beamed at the pixie. "Why, hello, little fellow."

"We already have two familiars in the library," Estelle protested. "What will Sylvester think? besides, I thought he had a family to get back to."

"Maybe he doesn't," I said. "It would explain why he attached himself to Tyler."

"I wouldn't object to him coming to live on the third floor with the other animals," said Cass. "But if Estelle wants him to work as her assistant, she's welcome to keep him."

"Jet?" I called, and the little crow flew down to land on my hand. "What d'you think of the pixie staying with us in the library?"

The pixie tilted his head at the crow, making chirping noises.

"He says he's sorry for putting a spell on me, partner!" Jet said. "He would be honoured to work for the library."

"How can you understand him?" I asked. "Can any of you?"

"Pixies speak their own language," said Estelle. "It'll be in one of our books, I'm sure."

Aunt Adelaide walked over. "What's he doing here?"

"I think he followed us home," I said. "And now he's taken a shine to Estelle."

"I'm not sure about this," Estelle said.

"Cass is right—you don't have your own familiar," I reminded her. "It's like Edwin said. The pixie obeyed Tyler because his orders appealed to his prank-loving nature, but he feels bad for what he did. I reckon he can be trained to be an assistant."

Aunt Adelaide grunted. "As long as he doesn't sabotage any more of our potions. After this week, I remember why I prefer working with books."

"You might have to do something about all the glitter, though," I added.

Aunt Candace gave the pixie an appraising look. "I've never studied a pixie before. Maybe he'll help me out with my new project."

"Oh, no you don't," said Estelle. "If he's staying, he'll be helping me."

"Better than Cupid, huh." I nudged her, and she grinned. "We can give him a trial run and see how he gets along. If that's okay with our other animals."

"Not me," said Sylvester, landing on the desk. "This is the thanks I get for helping you?"

"He can be trained, and we can always use another helper," I said. "Jet, what do you reckon?"

"I'd like a friend!" said Jet with enthusiasm.

Sylvester huffed, but everyone ignored him. The pixie perched on Estelle's shoulder and trailed its little fingers through her hair.

Estelle smiled. "Spark, do you want a tour of the library?"

My phone buzzed with a message from Xavier: *Want to head out for a walk?*

I hadn't had the opportunity to speak to him since we'd handed Tyler over to the police, so I responded with a yes.

Another message hit my phone a moment later... from Laney, my best friend from my life before I'd moved to the library. *So... who's the dreamy guy? Can I meet him?*

Xavier met me outside the library while I was still mulling over how to respond. "Hey, Rory."

"Hey." I looked up at him. "My best friend wants to meet you."

He arched a brow. "Should I know who this is?"

"Laney is a normal, so she can't come into the magical world," I said. "I don't like to tell her no, but if you're able to tone down the whole Reaper thing..."

"I can meet her." He flashed me a smile. "Don't you think I'm capable of pretending to be normal?"

Well, he *looked* a normal guy... if an inhumanly gorgeous one. "Maybe. More so than I am, these days."

"You should know, I've worked it out," Xavier said. "Why you can see into Death."

"Oh?" I asked warily. "Why is that?"

"When a Reaper develops a strong bond with a non-Reaper, they sometimes develop a connection," he said. "It's rare for Reapers to develop feelings for mortals, and vice versa, so there haven't been many studies done on it or anything, but it's not unheard of for a mortal who dates a Reaper to end up experiencing a milder version of our own link to the afterworld."

Oh. Now it made sense that I hadn't been able to see into Death before I'd met him, or even when we'd first been getting to know one another. "What does the Grim Reaper think?"

"He doesn't know," he said. "I think we should keep it quiet. But at least we have an explanation now."

"We do." I looked at my phone, which buzzed again. "What do you think, then?"

"I already met your family." He smiled. "I'm in your life for the long haul, Rory. I promise."

My heart skipped a beat, and I hit reply, sending a message to Laney. *Xavier would love to meet you. When are you free?*

ABOUT THE AUTHOR

Elle Adams lives in the middle of England, where she spends most of her time reading an ever-growing mountain of books, planning her next adventure, or writing. Elle's books are humorous mysteries with a paranormal twist, packed with magical mayhem.

She also writes urban and contemporary fantasy novels as Emma L. Adams.

Find Elle on Facebook at https://www.facebook.com/pg/ElleAdamsAuthor/

www.ingramcontent.com/pod-product-compliance
Lightning Source LLC
Chambersburg PA
CBHW020810190726
48285CB00006B/2232